LOVE, DEATH, AND ART

by

Doug McKim

SAME OLD STORY PRODUCTIONS

VICTOR FERUS, CEO and President

LOVE, DEATH, AND ART

Although this book takes place in my home turf of eastern Oregon, it was conceived and written almost entirely in Middle Tennessee, near the city of Nashville.

I dedicate this story to my friends and "adopted" family in Tennessee, who tolerated my occasional snotty, bratty, and immature behavior during the time I resided near the small, yet bustling community of Mount Juliet.

A special thank you to the Midgett clan, who allowed me to stay in their home for the duration of my stay there. I'll forever cherish their warmth, kindness, and generosity. This book would not be possible, had the Midgetts not allowed me an opportunity to pursue writing along with other activities throughout the Nashville region.

For their sacrifices on my behalf, I am eternally grateful.

1

It was a cold, rainy, nasty September day when I went on my last date with my ex-boyfriend, Danny O'Roarke.

It was Saturday, thank God, and no school! I spent most of that morning working on a pastel in my sketchbook. I hunched over a cluttered desk in my second-story bedroom, detailing the ferocious eyes and pointed snout of an angry, hungry, and man-eating dragon. I was also in a losing war with myself over this project, and dealt with an endless battle involving low self-esteem and confidence.

I was a high school senior in Nez Perce, a small town in northeastern Oregon, right along the Columbia River. I had absolutely no idea what I was gonna do, once Superintendent Tim Tanaka handed me my diploma, shook my hand, and wished me well in life. I was seventeen, and too busy still being a kid to even consider adulthood. I didn't wanna grow up! I was so fucking scared of it and truly scared of a lotta things! At that point, I never even held a real job after school, on weekends, or during summers. I usually just hung out in my bedroom, watching movies or working away in my sketchbook. I was way too shy and nervous to have my artwork displayed in public.

Those who had already saw some of my stuff told me I was a good artist. But, hell, I wasn't convinced of that.

I was and still am a huge fan of Frank Frazetta, Norman Rockwell, Maxfield Parrish, and Boris Vallejo. Anyone who ever visited my messy bedroom could tell, based on the posters which covered every inch of the four walls, and even a few tacked up on the ceiling! I had paperbacks and prints of *Conan the Barbarian, Carson of Venus, John Carter of Mars,* and *Tarzan of the Apes*. I also had tons of coffee table books, with biographies of those who I saw as artistic masters.

I had an actual movie poster of a Frazetta painting, from a movie that the Clint made a long time ago, titled *The Gauntlet*. It wasn't just a crappy reproduction, but an actual, real-life movie poster! Mom got it for me, when the old *Chief Joseph Theatre* had closed their doors for good, then sold a bunch of their stuff. Mom scrounged through their collection of movie posters, and found some she knew I'd like.

I also got *Excalibur,* the first "Conan" movie, *Full Metal Jacket, Apocalypse Now,* and a lot of other ones.

I always loved working with paint and pastels. I kinda-sorta-maybe got serious about it, during my Freshman year of high school. My art teacher, Ms. Goodwin, kept telling me to step out of my comfort zone, and really experiment with my projects. At first, I tried my hand at anime and manga. Then "Old Lady" Goodwin introduced me to the artists that I got to idolizing . . .. Frank, Norman, good old Boris. I wanted to be like these guys, while also trying to develop my own style. Even then, I didn't know if any of my artwork was any good, or "worth a shit," as Uncle Ray would say. I wanted to be worth a shit, and have other people brag on me and tell me how good I was, and stuff. I wanted to be good and all. Somehow, I never thought my artwork was worth a shit.

Old Lady Goodwin and Mom said I was good. My soon-to-be-ex-boyfriend Danny O'Roarke also said I was good. He said he wanted me to do the artwork for his books, once he got to be a big-shot writer. Anyways, neither Mom's, or Old Lady Goodwin's, or Danny's opinions didn't seem to matter. You kind-of-sort-of expect your mom, your teacher, or your boyfriend to say nice things. Uncle Ray always wondered where I got the idea for all "long-haired, crazy-assed shit" I drew and painted.

Anyways, Aunt Fran said I was good. She thought I'd be better if I drew and painted nature things, like squirrels and trees and deer and snow-covered, granite peaks, and all that other outdoorsy stuff. Uncle Ray and Aunt Fran wondered why I wasted my time and talent painting warriors, superheroes, knights in shining armor, damsels in distress, dragons, and monsters.

I tried to please everyone.... and usually ended up never pleasing myself.

Anyways, I was busy working on the eyes of the pastel dragon, when Mom hollered from downstairs, "Gerry.... Breakfast's ready!"

I sat up straight, stretched my back, took a deep breath, and pushed myself away from the desk. I wandered down a narrow stairway and into the dining room to find Mom, Uncle Ray, and Aunt Fran sitting around the table. They dug into their scrambled eggs, hash browns, sausage links, and coffee. I blundered on over to the table, and tried to enjoy my meal.

I say "tried" because I failed at most everything I done around Uncle Ray.

Right after Mom said, "Good morning," and Aunt Fran said, "Whatcha been doin' up there, Gerald? Nearly gave up on ya!" Uncle Ray said, "You gonna do something today that might be worth a shit?"

I tried not to get mad whenever Uncle Ray said that kind of stuff. He said it every morning, then let out a snicker like it was the first time he ever said it. Anyways, it never paid to get mad around Uncle Ray, because then he'd come back with something even more ornery, then laugh even harder. All getting mad did was to start fights between Uncle Ray, Aunt

Fran, and Mom. Aunt Fran always stuck up for me. Then Uncle Ray always came back with even something even more ornery, which made me nervous and upset.

I guess my looks and non-threatening manners gave Uncle Ray plenty of ammunition to use against me. I was, and still am, kind of a little guy, at five-two. Most of the people in my family were kind of little, even Uncle Ray. The only things big about him was his blustery voice, his thick, gray beard, and his fat ass. I had long, blonde hair, in a ponytail which hung way down between my scrawny shoulder blades. My hands were small, dainty, and uncalloused, a point which Uncle Ray always riled me up about. I was, and still am, prone to wearing sweaters or sweatshirts, shorts, and sandals, unlike the filthy work boots, *Lee* jeans, and denim shirts Ray thought I ought to wear.

Uncle Ray never saw the arts as work, or even as an occupation. For him, work was something you did outside in the hot, blazing sun, or in the dead of winter, even in sub-zero temperatures. Work hardened the muscles, tanned the skin, built character, and "goddamn it, made a man outa you!" He harped on my artwork, my clothes, my love of "high-falutin'" classical music, and not the old country songs he always listened to.

Worst of all, he bitched at the "sissy boy" ways in which I talked.

Well, I did and still do kind of talk in a bit of a high-pitched voice and lisp. I don't know what the hell I'm supposed to do about that. I tried to deepen my voice, get rid of the lisp, and act more "manly." It made me look and sound dumber than I already am.

Worst of all was when Ray wondered when I was gonna get myself a girlfriend.

I never have had, and I never will have, a girlfriend. I like girls and women as friends, but nothing more. I never been with a girl or a woman, when it comes to the nasty. Just about everyone I knew, including Uncle Ray, knew I wasn't into women. They already figured that I'd never get myself a girlfriend or a wife.

Mom and Aunt Fran knew I was gay, even before I knew I was and still am gay.

Anyways, it never paid to get mad, whenever Uncle Ray asked if I was gonna be worth a shit. My only response was to slap on a phony, stupid-assed grin, and say, "Depends on what you mean by being worth a shit."

"Like doing work!" hollered Ray, with a cocky smile. "I mean *work…* a goddamn, honest day's, man's work! I mean by helping me work on that goddamn truck out there in the barn, or nailing down that loose tin on the toolshed!"

"Now, Ray," harped Fran. "You know darned good and well you'll never got to working on that broken-down, old *GMC!*"

"Who says I ain't gonna?" argued Ray.

"I said you ain't gonna!" Fran snapped back. "Damn thing's been sit-tin' out there for neared fifteen years. Engine's blowed up, windshield wip-ers and headlights don't work. Quit workin' long before you quit drivin' it. Damned truck ain't worth the mendin'. So don't start on it." Fran gave me a look. "And quit givin' Gerald a hard time. You know as well as I do he ain't no car mechanic, so there ain't no point buggin' 'em about it."

"Well," growled Ray, "least he oughta be doing is going out to feed the animals, while I go out and fix the roof on that shed."

"Now Ray," scolded Fran. "You won't do no such thing as fix the roof on that old shed. Ain't nothin' in there to fret over."

"I got a couple of fools sticks and some rakes in there. Don't want them getting wet and ruined, do ya?"

"*Aw!*" groaned Fran. "Just haul them tools to the barn, then get one of the neighbors to come over and tear down that old tool shed. You done had one heart attack earlier this year. Tryna do? Go out and have another, maybe worse this time?"

"Ain't gonna have another goddamn heart attack!" hollered Ray, his voice echoing through the house.

"That'll due to tell," said Fran, her piercing eyes practically drilling holes through Uncle Ray.

"Oh hell, might have me another heart attack, at that," mumbled Ray, with a smartass grin. "If I gotta keep living with an old sow like you."

"I'll go out and feed the animals!" I spoke up, to change the subject and keep Aunt Fran from strangling Uncle Ray, which would be worse than any heart attack. Anyways, I kind of liked feeding the animals, mainly the rabbits and chickens. "I'll go out and feed them, Uncle Ray. Don't you worry, sir. Then I'll go upstairs and work on my dragon a little more, before I go on my date."

"Who ya datin'?" asked Ray. "Mexican woman or negro girl? Hope she's pretty. Might getcha down and make a man outa you..."

"Ray!" screeched Fran, mad as a wet hen.

"Aw, hell, just giving 'em a hard time!" defended Ray, with a mean-looking grin. "So... Who do ya gotta date with?"

I cleared my throat, then looked over at Mom and Aunt Fran before giving an answer. "Dan.... Danny O'Roarke," I said.

"*Who?*" asked Ray.

"Danny O'Roarke," I whispered.

Uncle Ray gave Mom a dirty look, like it was her fault that I was and still am gay, or something.

Aunt Fran wagged a finger at Uncle Ray, to get him to shut up about it, and not give me a hard time. Then she pointed at his dish, so he'd get back to eating his eggs, taters, and sausage. Aunt Fran might have been a short, plump, homely little woman, even shorter than me. But she had a way to get Uncle Ray to shut up and do what he was told.

I couldn't help but to like, and still like, that grey-haired old woman.

Mom didn't say much. She was a nurses' aide in one of the old folks' home down in Hermiston, and never did say much after one of the residents got real bad sick, died, or something horrible like that.

From what I was told, two of her favorite old folks kicked off during the night, and Mom had a bad habit of getting all worked up and upset and teary-eyed and mushy and all that. On that rainy Saturday morning, I thought she'd up and cry her eyes out or something. Nothing I could say or do would keep her from getting real sad about stuff. She gave me a stupid, phony-assed grin, trying to pretend like she was okay, which she wasn't. The look in her eyes made me wonder if she was on the verge of a nervous breakdown. Nothing I could say or do would keep her from that, neither.

Anyways, Uncle Ray ate his eggs, taters, and sausage, and didn't have much to say, or ask if I was dating a Mexican, a "negro", Danny O'Roarke, or the *Good Humor Man.*

When I got done eating, I ran upstairs to fetch a hoodie sweatshirt. Then I ran outside to feed the animals, like what Uncle Ray wanted me to. When I got back downstairs, Aunt Fran was still at the table, drinking coffee while smoking a *Winston.* She was busy chewing Ray out for smoking too many *Lucky Strikes,* drinking too much *Henry Weinhard's Private Reserve,* and working too hard around the place.

He'd usually end up chewing her out for smoking too much herself, while sitting on her fat ass all day, drinking coffee by the gallons, and gluing her eyes to the TV. Every day, Fran watched old Western shows like *The Virginian,* followed by *Gunsmoke, The Big Valley, Bonanza,* and *The Rifleman.* More often than not, Uncle Ray watched *Lonesome Dove* at least three or four times a year.

Uncle Ray and Aunt Fran hardly watched anything but Westerns. Nothing but Westerns. It was also that way with their DVDs and old VCR tapes. They kept all their movies in a converted gun cabinet, in a dusty corner of the front room.

Anyways, Aunt Fran quit harping at Uncle Ray, and instead decided to harp at me. "Ain't you gonna wear somethin' better than *that,* outside?"

"No," I said, fetching a pair of jersey gloves from the closet. "Why?"

"Gonna freeze out there!" griped Fran, eyeing my scrawny bare legs with anger, worry, and contempt. "Get back upstairs, and get some clothes on!"

"It's awright," I said, with a slight blush and a nervous grin. "It'll be okay. No need to worry…"

"It's cold outside!" Fran hollered, looking through the dusty window above the kitchen sink. "Rained all night last night! Couldn't you hear it, beating down on the tin roof over yer head? Wind's blowin' real hard, too! Go on, get yerself back upstairs, and get on some clothes before you die from the damp!"

Uncle Ray didn't say much. He just gave me an awkward sort of look, glad it was me getting picked on and not him. He took one last sip of his coffee, and one last puff of his cigarette. "Guess I better get outside and get busy nailing that loose tin on the toolshed," he said.

Putting on a black, worn-out *Remington* cap, he escaped through the darkened pantry, lined with jars of canned apples and peaches, then headed outside.

"Don't get too busy workin' on that damn thing," warned Fran, her raspy voice changing from a high-pitched one to a low one, with every other word. "We need you around here more than any damn fools stick or rake you got stored in that tool shed."

I thought strongly of making good an escape, while I still could. But before I could get to the front room door, Fran hollered out, "*Ah-ah-ah!* You get right back over here, and put on some clothes, before you go outside and feed them animals."

I rolled my eyes back, sighed, then tried to convince Fran that a little bit of rain and cold air wouldn't kill me.

"Gerald O'Fearna!" screeched Fran, snapping her fingers while pointing at the stairway. "Get your butt upstairs and get some clothes on, then you feed them animals!"

Well, there was no point in getting mad at the old woman. She was right, and if you don't believe me just ask her.

I headed up to my bedroom, took off my sandals, put on a pair of ratty old *Nikes,* replaced my corduroy shorts for a pair of faded, cut-off jeans, then sneaked outside before Aunt Fran, or Mom, or God Almighty could harp at me some more.

Mom and me moved upstairs of Uncle Ray and Aunt Fran's farmhouse, about a mile or so east of Nez Perce. This happened about a week after my dad, who was also named Gerald O'Fearna, died of a heart attack one night while working at the McNary Dam, on the Columbia. When we lost Dad, we lost just about everything, including a *Dodge Ram* he was making payments on, and the nice house we just got. Heart attacks are like a big deal on both sides of my family. Imagine I'll have one before I'm fifty. I'm not saying I'm looking forward to it, I'm just saying I'll have one, like it or not.

Anyways, as a result of Dad dying suddenly, Mom and me moved upstairs of Ray and Fran's place. Mom told Ray and Fran that we'd get our own place, when she got back on her feet. That was about three years ago. I guess Mom never got back on her feet, because we didn't get our own place yet. Mom still pitched in by getting groceries, cooking a few meals, and doing a few chores here and there. I did what I could to help out, like feed animals and help Uncle Ray do little fix-em-up jobs. That is, when Fran wasn't harping at us about it.

Mom was in her late-thirties. Already, touches of grey lined her dishwater, blonde hair. A few wrinkles creased around her eyes, and across her forehead. Fran said it came from getting all worked up about Dad dying, thoughts of getting back on her feet, and fretting about how we'd make it without Dad. Mom never worked much before Dad died. He didn't want her to. He figured it was his duty to go out and make money. Mainly, Mom worked around the house, raised me, and volunteered here and there.

After Dad died, Mom didn't do much at first except cry her eyes out, and worry herself silly. Finally, she took some CNA classes and ended up working at an old folk's home in Hermiston. She usually worked swing shifts, and sometimes graveyard. Mom worked as much as she could, and put money aside for a new place, when she got back on her feet. Uncle Ray fretted that I ought to be helping her out, by working summer vacations and on weekends. Of course, it all had to be man's work, and not in a store or in a restaurant, and not doing paintings or pastels, which wasn't work and wasn't worth a shit anyways.

Anyways, Ray sometimes claimed I was allergic to work, since I never learned what the word meant. Fran stood up for me, and said that I worked plenty by feeding the animals and keeping Ray from having another heart attack…. "maybe worse this time."

I headed outside and wandered the fifty yards or so to the barn, the same barn where Uncle Ray kept the old GMC pickup he'd been wanting to fix up for fifteen years. By now, hay dust covered the old, late-70s model rig. It was a four door. The driver's side window had been kept open, where the rig was left sitting. Rain, snow, wind, and pretty much everything else pretty much destroyed the car seats and everything else in there, to the point where I wondered why Ray would want to fix it up. Ray hauled firewood, furniture, hogs and hay in the GMC. By now, chickens had got in the cab and crapped all over the seats and dashboard and stuff.

Rabbit hutches lined one side of the barn. Once I showed up, several hens, a couple of roosters, a few ducks and geese and the rabbits all seemed happy and eager to see me, to the point where I got kind of mobbed when they ran, walked, or waddled over to greet me.

I opened up a fifty-pound sack of *Cenex* grain that Uncle Ray picked up at the local co-op, and dumped it in a barrel. I gave each rabbit a bunch of alfalfa and grain, then scattered pellets of grain on the ground for the chickens, ducks, and geese to fight over. I then filled a couple of V-shaped feeders that Ray hand-made from two-by-fours and plywood. The chickens flocked to the feeders, and went nuts over their food. I fetched a water hose from a large nail hanging from a corner post in the barn, then filled up a couple of plastic and aluminum canisters. I then went around and gave each rabbit some water.

Once I got done at the barn, I went to an old wooden whiskey barrel, where barley soaked in water for three hogs who lived in a nearby smokehouse. The smokehouse must've been at least fifty years old, if not older. It was sure an ugly old building. The smokehouse was covered with holes, where woodpeckers pecked on it. It teetered over to one side, and I expected it to fall over one of these days, during a bad windstorm.

I put the soak in a five-gallon, plastic bucket, then headed to the smokehouse where three pigs oinked and squealed in joy.

I managed to get my chores done, before the next heavy downpour of rain. However, when I headed to the porch, the rain started up again, and I ended up running to keep from getting drenched.

I saw Uncle Ray sitting at a bench on the front porch. He had a cigarette in one hand, a beer in the other, and a lip full of *Copenhagen.* He waved at me as I dashed over to him, and got awful wet in the process. "Get yer scrawny ass over here!" he hollered, with an ornery grin.

Thunder rumbled and lightning striked from the west. Ray took a drag from his smoke and yelled, "Ain't doin' no goddamn good getting' yer ass wet in all that mud and rain!"

I jumped onto the porch, and sat next to Ray on the bench. Although he harassed and bullyragged me up one side and down the other, I still couldn't help but to like that old bastard... even when I hated him.

Ray reached down to a six-pack sitting on the floor next to him, and handed me a bottle of Weinhard's.

I kind of looked Ray in the eye, and shrugged nervously. "Aww..." I whispered. "I dunno if Mom or Aunt Fran would want me drinking...."

"Take the goddamn thing!" hollered Ray, sitting the brew in my lap. "What them hussies in there, with all their gossip and sewing, don't know sure as shit won't hurt 'em! Take the goddamn thing!"

I took a quick look through the window behind me. Sure enough, there was Mom and Aunt Fran, plopped down on the couch, chatting back and forth by the warm fireplace. On the TV, Matt Dillon got done killing another bad guy on "Gunsmoke."

I cautiously twisted the top off the bottle of beer and took a sip.

"Get anything done out there that was worth a shit?" asked Ray.

"Fed all the animals," I said, starting to relax and enjoy myself, as rain beat down on the tin roof above.

"Get 'em fed up right?"

"Yes, sir, that I did!"

"They thank you proper for what you done for 'em?" asked Ray.

"Hell, they couldn't think me enough!" I said, with a half-way grin.

"Then, by god, you deserve the bus stop." Ray handed me a cigarette. "While them ladies sit on their ass in the warm house, talkin' trash about the neighbors, we'll sit out here and do what men do, which don't amount to a hell of a lot."

I really didn't like smoking. Truth was, I couldn't stand cigarettes! Lucky Strikes were especially horrible, mostly the ones without filters. But who was I to argue with Uncle Ray? He was gonna win, anyways.

Anyways, the chores were all done, the ground was getting good and wet for the winter, and I was feeling awful good about things, under the circumstances. I'd rather be indoors working on my pastel, whether it was worth a shit or not. I also had to get ready for what would be my last date with my soon-to-be-ex-boyfriend, Danny O'Roarke.

Uncle Ray wanted me to do men's work and guy stuff like drink and smoke and cuss and fart. I drank and smoked and cussed and farted, all right, but I really hated chewing tobacco. The beer was one thing, the cigarette another, and the cussing and farting something else. Chewing tobacco was flat-out disgusting and gross, and wasn't worth a shit.

Uncle Ray and I sat on the bench, listening to rain beat on the tin roof, as we quietly looked out across the grey, foggy, cloudy world before us.

Seemed Uncle Ray wasn't able to catch a good breath, and even looked more pale than normal. At some point, he got to coughing so bad I thought he'd kick off, any minute. I never told him how worried I was. He'd just tell me to shut my goddamn mouth, mind my own goddamn business, and go to Hell.

Something just told me that he wasn't doing good at all.

Anyways, all we did was sit out there, staring off across the distance. Uncle Ray and Aunt Fran owned about two-hundred acres back behind the house, and about fifty acres across the highway, which ended at the banks of the Columbia River. There weren't much trees or brush out there, except on the foothills of southeast Washington. Most of that was just ugly desert country, under the jurisdiction of the BLM or some other damned Commie organization, as Ray called it.

Ray and Fran owned lots of land, but they never worked it much anymore. Mainly, it was leased out to cattle ranchers and alfalfa farmers. Way in the back, behind the house, was a small apple orchard. Ray never done much with that, neither. For the most part, he sold the apples to a family known as the Ortegas. Old Man Ortega was a former migrant from down Mexico way, who made some money and worked real hard for farms and ranches around Hermiston, Milton-Freewater, the Tri-Cities, and Walla Walla. Now, most of his kids and grandkids worked at food processing plants or at *Wal-Mart*. Ray and Fran knew the Ortegas for thirty years or more, and they liked them real good. Only thing is, Ray badmouthed them, because "the wet-back sons of bitches won't talk good American," which made him awful mad sometimes.

Uncle Ray and Aunt Fran weren't just my aunt and uncle. They were Mom's aunt and uncle too, which made them a lot older than me. Ray was in his seventies and, as Fran was always quick to point out, had one heart attack already. Fran never had a heart attack yet. She was just working on it, from constant nagging and fretting and worry and cigarettes.

Neither Ray nor Fran did much work now, and mainly looked after two or three acres around the house. They had already sold most of their farm equipment, like tractors, wagons, and balers. They were thinking about selling most of their land, to those already leasing it, including "them wet-back Spicks," the Ortegas. Still, they aimed on leaving part of it to family. They even said they'd leave a small part of it to Mom and me, whether we got on our feet or not. Mom always thanked Ray and Fran for taking us in, but said she wanted to get on her feet on her own.

Anyways, Ray and I just sat there, smoking and drinking while looking off in the distance, at much of nothing at all. Despite the crappy weather, there were a few damned fool fishermen in small boats on the river, trying to catch fish. They were probably catching colds, while also getting good and drunk. Ray liked to fish all right, but had more sense than you take a boat out in the fog, wind, and rain. He figured it'd serve those knotheads right to capsize and float away, either to drown or get ground up in the McNary Dam, and end up as fish bait.

I got done with my first beer, and quietly got me another. Finally, Uncle Ray spoke up. "Anybody at school give you a hard time?"

Even under the calming, moron-inducing effects of the Henry's, a jolt ran through my body. Even after trying hard not to, I couldn't help but to blush. I knew what Ray was getting at. I tried real hard to play dumb. "Whadda ya mean?" I asked.

Ray looked for a way to get his words out. "Aw, you know," he whispered, like he was kind of ashamed to bring it up. "Do they give you a hard time.... Y' know.... For the way you are?"

I thought about getting mad at the question. What the hell good was getting mad? Anyways, there was no real orneriness or mean-spirited sound in Ray's voice. Seemed like he was truly concerned about me. Even then, I really didn't know how to answer the question. "Ah.... Sometimes.... I dunno.... I guess," I said, nervously.

"So, what're ya gonna do about it?" Ray asked, gawking at a big black bull, standing a few hundred yards away on the Washington side.

"I don't do anything," I said, anxiously. "I just kind of ignore it."

This wasn't entirely true. How the hell can you ignore it, when all you hear are words like "homo," "queer," "faggot," and even worse things? Truth is, these names cut me clear to the bone! I only pretend they don't bother me. It was getting harder and harder to pretend. Truth is, these words hurt more and more, with each passing day!

Sons of bitches....

Dirty, goddamn fucking sons of bitches....

"Get into fights with 'em?" asked Ray, quietly.

I didn't answer. I couldn't answer! What the hell good was answering? I was just a shrimpy kid, and only weighed a little more than a hundred pounds. What the hell good was fighting? Just so I could get my ass beat? I wasn't a fighter! I never learned how to fight. All I knew how to do was paste on some phony-assed grin, and act like those words never hurt me. The truth is, those words hurt me and still hurt me. All the fucking time.

Though I tried to hold them back, a few teardrops dripped from my eyes. The more I tried to stop them, the worse they got. I held my head down low, staring at my feet along with the porch floor, its paint fading from being walked over all the time. I looked away from Ray, to hide the pain. It didn't work. Ray knew I was all worked up over the question.

Guess I was, and still am too much of a weakling and a wimp.

Uncle Ray spit out a wad of spit out into the rain, as he flipped a cigarette butt into the wet ground. A stupid red hen, who was hiding under the porch, ran out in hopes that the cigarette was some sort of food. The hen pecked at the smoldering butt, and found out it wasn't good to eat. It just kind of looked up at Ray in some sort of betrayal, then ran back under the porch.

Ray fetched himself another smoke, along with a *Bic* lighter. He coughed a time or two, then took a deep drag. "Had me a cousin once, kinda like you," he said, hoping what he wanted to say wouldn't be overheard from Mom or Aunt Fran. "Guess he kinda took to likin' guys, too. 'Course, this was more'n fifty years ago, when guys like you and him weren't inclined to get it out in the open. Back then, it was best keepin' it to yerself, and not tell nobody about it."

I looked over at Uncle Ray, and didn't say anything. I was more interested in what he had to say next.

"My cousin, Sid," Ray went on. "Yer cousin, too, if he was still around."

Ray stopped to yawn and stretch his aching back.

"About the time Sid got to be yer age," he continued, "he got to hangin' around a fella a lot older'n you, around thirty I reckon. Well, before ya knew it, them two got to messin' around. Tried keepin' it outa everybody's business, and keep it to themselves. But what the hell good did that do? Hell, a blind man could tell what was going on! Well, Sid, he kept on hangin' around with that fella, stayin' out later and later at night. Pretty soon, he was pretty much livin' with that fella, up in some shrimpy little trailer, barely big enough for just one bed. You figure it out."

Ray stopped for a moment or two.

"Well, as you can imagine," he went on, "Uncle Dick didn't take too well to that. Dick was Sid's old man, y' see. Well, Uncle Dick went to fetch Sid back from that fella's trailer, late one night. Didn't even knock on the door. He just let himself in. Caught Sid and that fella goin' at it on that tiny little bed." Ray took a deep breath, and let it out in a raspy cough. "Dick headed back to his car for an old 30.06 he kept in there all the time, went back, and shot poor Sid and that other fella. Killed 'em both, deader'n hell, right then and there. When he got done killin' them two, he drove out somewhere out on the Diagonal Road, finished a bottle of some damn rotgut whiskey, stuck the barrel of that .06 in his mouth, and . . ."

Ray ended the story, right then and there. Didn't need to go on.

"Holy shit," I gasped.

I never once heard that story before, and never even knew that an Uncle Dick or a cousin Sid even existed! But I could understand why no one in the family ever talked about it. Of course, I wondered if they talked about it between themselves, where no one else could hear it, and just kind of kept it to themselves.

"Just don't want you to end up like that, that's all," mumbled Ray. "Can't understand fellas like you and Sid. Ain't even sure if I care to go along with it! That don't mean I want you to end up that way. Hell, no. Don't expect me to go along with what yer doin'. But if I ever hear of any- one bullyraggin' you or hasslin' you over it, then they'll have to tangle with me." Ray put his hand on my shoulder. "I don't get fellas like you. I don't like it, don't care to go along with it. But, by god, we're family, and I won't stand for anyone givin' family a hard time about nothin'. Got that?"

Another teardrop or two dripped from my eyes. Uncle Ray sure wasn't the nicest guy in the world. I sometimes wanted to land right in the middle of him, and tell him exactly how mad he got me. But when he told me that horrible story, along with his willingness to stand up for me, if for no reason other than us being kin, about made me cry like a baby. Ray could be a real asshole, a fucking jerk! But, at that moment I was moved by what he just told me.

"You feed them animals real good and proper?" asked Ray, with a twinkle in his eye.

"Sure did," I said. "They were real happy with me. If you don't believe me, go ask them!"

"By god, I'll take yer word for it," said Ray. "No need for me to head out there and see if yer tellin' me the truth. I'll take yer word for it. Now get yerself indoors and get yerself ready for that date." Ray reached into his pants pocket for a bit of money that he slapped in the palm of my hand. "Better take this," he said. "Never know. Might come in handy."

I looked at the money that Ray just gave me.

It was a twenty.

I shook my head and handed it back to Ray. "Naw, I can't take this," I said, feeling kind of ashamed and embarrassed. "I really don't think I need it. . ."

"Take it, goddamn it!" hollered Ray. "Take it before I stick it in yer ear, yer eyes, or someplace else!"

I reluctantly slipped the money into my shorts pocket. "Thanks," I said. "I'll be real smart with it, and try not to spend it in one place."

"Hope you and that other fella have a good time." Ray gave me an evil eye. "Don't bother tellin' me how good a time you and him got. I don't wanna know."

With that, I shook Ray's hand, got up from the bench, then sneaked indoors to get ready for my date with Danny O'Roarke.

I also took the time to wash my mouth out with *Listerine,* to get rid of the beer and cigarette smell. That way, neither Mom nor Aunt Fran would have nothing to harp at me about.

2

I tried getting back to work on my pastel of the dragon. But by then, I just wasn't in the mood anymore. Guess that story Uncle Ray told me about his cousin Sid, along with my date with Danny, got me out of the mood, somehow. Anyways, I looked at what I did so far on the pastel, and wondered if it was worth a shit, and thought maybe it wasn't.

I almost thought about shredding the pastel into a million pieces. I wondered if any of my artwork was worth a shit, and thought people only said nice things out of kindness. I really started thinking that I'd never be worth a shit, either as an artist or as a person, and fear nearly overwhelmed me.

Then thoughts of me throwing myself off a bridge into the Columbia River crept into my mind.

Screw that! I was and still am too scared to take my own life. Tomorrow would always be another day. Sometimes, it seemed a bit brighter, somehow. Sure, I might decide to do something stupid like kill myself, change my mind right after I took the jump, then end up dead anyways.

I put my scrapbook in a shelf above my desk, went to the dresser, and looked for some nice clothes to meet Danny in. I didn't want to be too formal, but didn't want to be a slob, neither.

Although I'd get hollered at by Mom and Aunt Fran over it, I decided to go with a pair of cargo shorts. They weren't too baggy, but not too revealing either. They only showed an inch or two above my knees. I also picked out a blue sweatshirt with an image of my school mascot, the *Nez Perce Warriors*.

There were some in town who wanted to change the mascot from "Warriors" to "Peacemakers." But that new name doesn't sound too ferocious or intimidating, especially not on the football field or wrestling mat.

Finally, I picked out a thin, long-sleeved tee-shirt to wear underneath. I also went with a pair of white, athletic socks, and my nicest hiking shoes. I aimed to walk into town to meet Danny. I already knew that Mom and Aunt Fran would screech at me for not wearing something nicer or warmer, figuring the weather. Still, it called for partly-cloudy skies in the afternoon, and no more rain until about midnight . . . maybe. I didn't want to freeze on the way to town and back, but I hated feeling hot and sweaty. Even if Mom offered to drive me into town, to a local burger joint called *The Warriors Den,* I still preferred to hoof it.

"The Warriors Den" was named after the school mascot, and was a popular hang-out for kids. The Warriors Den sounded better than "The Peacemakers Den" which doesn't sound very good to me, at all.

I took a hot shower, then got into my clean clothes. I made sure to use plenty of stick deodorant, so I wouldn't stink too bad. I combed my hair back and tied it down into a ponytail, then brushed my teeth.

Later on, I took a look at my small, scrawny image in the mirror. I wasn't too bad of a looking guy. I sure wasn't ruggedly handsome. I still looked a bit young for my age, even kind of feminine. My jaw seemed kind of round and childlike. I had no facial hair, but instead patchy spots of peach fuzz on my upper lip and chin. My eyes were a bright blue, deep-set, even kind of beady. My cheeks were dimpled, which pleased Mom no end! My nose was pointy but, thank God, not pugged. My legs were too light and pale for my liking. I never tanned, but sunburned really good. I wanted to be taller and darker.

Some people, especially old women and girls, said I looked petite and *cute*. I didn't know whether to be flattered or insulted by that.

Well, I can dream of being a bit more macho. To this day, I'm still not very dark or tall. Think I'd rather be tall, dark, and ruggedly handsome than be petite and cute.

Anyways, after I got done primping and obsessing over myself in the mirror, I fetched my Nez Perce Warriors baseball cap and headed downstairs. It was only a matter of time before Mom and Aunt Fran would fret, worry, and gripe, while Uncle Ray would go out of his way to make some smartass comment over me.

What I expected is pretty much what I got.

As I blundered into the front room, I found everybody sitting around, sipping coffee, smoking cigarettes, and watching *Little House on the Prairie*. There was enough tobacco smoke in there to make someone think the place was some sort of Republican convention. I braced myself for the "reviews," which usually made me scared, anxious, nervous, or a combination of all three.

"Well, hell, if that don't beat all!" roared Uncle Ray, treating my arrival like it was cause of a celebration, or a sad excuse of a comedy routine. "All lit up like a Christmas tree, and here it ain't yet Halloween!"

"Gerald O'Fearna! Get back upstairs and put some clothes on!" screeched Aunt Fran, staring at my shorts with frustration and anger. "Tryna die of the cold, y' young damn fool? Don'tcha know the wind's blowin' outside, and its freezin' like hell? Expectin' a frost by mornin'. Go get some clothes on, if yer gonna be walkin' into town!"

I looked away from Aunt Fran, to avoid her mean look and frown. I glanced over to a gun cabinet, in a dark corner of the front room. My attention floated over a couple of hunting rifles, one shotgun, and a *Dan Wesson* 357 Magnum, hanging from a leather holster. My cheeks altered to a fiery blush. "It's awright," I mumbled, with a moronic chuckle. "I plan to walk pretty fast, so..."

"Get some clothes on!" harped Fran, getting madder and madder by the minute. "Ain't you got sense enough than to dress better'n that, in the wind and rain? I swear, kids these days ain't got a lick of sense! Here he is, damn neared a grown man, and still he dresses like some half-witted boy on his way to Sunday School!"

"Want me to drive you to town?" whined Mom, certain that I'd come to a tragic and untimely end on my way to Nez Perce. "Here, let me get a jacket, and I'll drive..."

"I'll be okay, Mom!" I said, both amused and put-off by the grief, despair, and sorrow which I brought to the house. "I got my phone with me, so if anything happens I'll call you, just in case . . ."

"Ain't you afraid of freezin' them scrawny legs?" moped Fran. "Can't understand why kids think they gotta wear shorts all the time. Tryna do? *Advertise?* Ain't nobody under the age of twenty-one got any sense, than to wear shorts in this kinda weather..."

I felt myself getting kind of angry with Aunt Fran, and just about everybody else. Seemed I couldn't do anything right around them, without catching the Wrath of God, Aunt Fran, or Uncle Ray. Neither a day nor a decision went by where I wouldn't have to hear about it. It was my life, my body, my walk into town, and my shorts!

I started to chuckle, even as I thought about strangling someone .... Mainly someone named Ray, Fran, or both. Seemed if they weren't cussing me out, they'd be cussing each other out, about one thing or another. Half-witted boy or not, the walk into Nez Perce would either an enjoyable workout, or the death of me. One way or the other, it was my choice.

"Sure you don't want me to give you a ride?" asked Mom, on the verge of a nervous breakdown, along with the cardiac arrest she was already suffering from two old folks kicking off in the old folks' home.

"I'm sure, Mom," I said, with a touch of sarcasm. "It's not like I haven't walked to town before, and in a lot worse weather than this…"

Mom got a pained expression on her face, while Aunt Fran gave me the evil eye, while undoubtedly casting a terrible spell upon my everlasting soul.

"I'll call you if I need anything," I said, opening the front door which eventually lead me to town, or a fate worse than death. "I'll be okay, I promise." With a grin, I added, "Unless I get kidnapped or something."

Mom bit her bottom lip, as both eyes revealed impending doom for her one and only child.

"Serve you right, getting kidnapped," said Fran, shaking her head. "The way yer dressed, looks like yer wantin' to get picked up by some pervert. But, y' might as well get a move on it. Ain't nothin' more I can say about it. I'll keep my mouth shut, from now on. Ain't got nothin' more to say about it."

"Aw, y' never know," said Uncle Ray, just daring me to yell, holler, scream or whine in useless protest. "Some old Mexican woman or negro gal might take 'em to her place. Hell, y' never know. Might even make a man outa him."

With that, I stepped outside, shut the door behind me, and headed off to what would be my last date with my soon-to-be-ex-boyfriend, Danny O'Roarke.

3

My walk into Nez Perce that afternoon wasn't too bad. Highway 730, which kind of snaked along the river on the Oregon side, was wet and slippery. I'm glad I wore my good old "clod stompers," as Uncle Ray called them. They had thick soles and a nice tread on the bottom. They'd keep your feet warm in the winter, cool in the summer, and dry in the snow and rain. Although a school bus came by the house every weekday morning, I preferred walking to school, even in crummy weather.

Walking is cheaper than counseling, booze, or pills. Whenever I'm walking, nobody gives me shit. I enjoy my own company, and get to soak in blissful solitude, clean air, and sunshine. I'm not putting up with somebody's piss-poor attitude or bullshit!

A lot of people probably think I'm crazy, because I like walking. I finally got my driver's license in my early-twenties, because I ended up with a job which forced me into it. I never liked driving, especially in a maddening rush hour commute between the suburbs and inner cities. Give me a bike, a month's pass on a bus, or a pleasant walk somewhere, I'm one happy camper! Hopping in a car, and fighting traffic each and every day in and out of some huge metropolis, is nonsense. Don't anybody believe in mass transit or carpooling, for chrissakes? Would it kill anybody to go on a hike, or ride a bike sometimes?

And then they bitch about getting fat and breathing polluted air!

Anyways, it held off raining as I wandered along the two-lane, blacktop highway into Nez Perce. There were few boaters out on the water, braving the wet, clammy day. The breeze wasn't too bad. At first, my bare legs felt the damp and chill of the cool air. The farther and faster I walked, the easier it got. I started out at a slow pace, which picked up and gathered steam. In no time, I was really hoofing it, and I really liked the grey, overcast skies and rustic colors of fall. What an adventure! There weren't too many cars on the road, so I was able to relish these few moments to myself.

Most drivers who passed me by smiled and waved. A few stopped to offer me a ride. That was okay. I was having too good a time to ruin a fun walk. Not that I always minded taking rides, or jawing with neighbors from town.

Ray, Fran, and Mom had a ton of pals, some who were closer than family. Most of them didn't mind me being the way I was, and still am. If they minded, they sure didn't say anything about it, or harp at me, or remind me that I was destined to burn in the fiery pits of Hell for being that way.

A few folks insisted on me taking a ride, to avoid getting soaked or dying from the rain and cold. At least they were nice about it, and never raised a fuss like Mom or Aunt Fran.

The only ones who got nasty with me that afternoon was Frankie Hulse, and some of his chums.

I knew most of these jerks from all my years of going to school in Nez Perce. Frankie and his pals were about the same age as me, and also seniors in high school.

Frankie never was nice. He was athletic, maybe smarter, and better looking than me. His old man was a big-wig for *Bonneville*, and the family had bucks. Lots of bucks, and didn't mind showing off all the nice stuff money can buy.

Frankie was well over six feet tall, and played quarterback in football. He had black hair, a chiseled jaw, high cheek bones, and bright blue eyes that put movie idols to shame. He lifted weights, and often ran more miles a day than what I walked.

Personally, I really don't like running, unless there's something awful after me.

Anyways, Frankie was never nice, and got less so as time went on. When he was younger, Frankie called me names like "weakling," "wimp," and "weakling." Later, it became "homo" and "faggot." Now, it was stuff like "buttfucker," "cocksucker," and "asslick."

It got even worse, but enough about that.

Anyways, Frankie and some of his pals rode by in a fancy, red *Chevy* pickup. The minute they saw me, they got all stupid, with mean looks on their faces. They hurled insults, as well as a few beer cans and bottles at me, before speeding off and leaving skid marks on the road. A *Garth Brooks* song blasted from the stereo, as mud and gravel scattered at me.

I pretended like it didn't bother me, though it did and still does. Anyways, like what the song said, Frankie and his pals had friends in low places.

Anyways, Nez Perce, Oregon, was a small town of about seven-thousand people, who lived along the Columbia River, real close to the McNary Dam. Many of the folks here worked for Bonneville, farmed, ranched, or worked in restaurants, bars, clubs, stores, or taverns in town. Some were retired.

In the past few years, a bunch of Californians started moving in. The older folks in Nez Perce accused them of trying to take over.

I had yet to meet too many Oregonians who had use for Californians.

Uncle Ray called them "no-account, know-it-all, nosey, busy-body sons of bitches." He said worse things, but I won't repeat them.

Anyways, Ray and Fran wanted to keep Oregon just the way it was when they were younger, when no one gave you a hard time about owning guns, logging or mining, or what you did or didn't do on your own place. Ray and Fran wanted to keep things simple, and it seemed the longer things went on, the less simple it got. More and more people moved into Nez Perce, and more and more it changed. Frankie Hulse wasn't born in Nez Perce. I think he was from Joseph or Enterprise, or one of them other places in Wallowa County. It didn't matter. He still acted like a Californian.

Years back, Ray used to gripe about all the Mexicans in town, and there were lots of them, too. They were either migrants, or the kids or grandkids of migrants. They first came to Washington and Oregon to work the fields and orchards. They saved their money, then took what they made back down south of the border.

Soon, the migrants decided to stay, until Nez Perce's Mexican population almost equaled that of the whites.

I really didn't mind the Mexicans. I couldn't remember a time when there wasn't a bunch of them, already. Neither Ray nor Fran were that fond of the Mexicans, because they tended to cling around their own kind, and rarely "talked good American," unless they had to. Even then, Ray and Fran had more use of the Mexicans, than they did Californians. In Ray's mind, most Mexicans weren't afraid of hard work, ran good, honest businesses, and treated others with respect and kindness. Ray always bought gas and oil from a nearby *Shell* station, owned by a couple of young Mexican brothers, because they treated him extra-special nice, and he wanted to return the favor. He and Fran also went to a Mexican restaurant on Eleventh Street in Hermiston, because it served the best enchiladas for a darn good price. I think it was also because Ray took a fancy to a pretty young Mexican waitress in there, but enough about that.

Anyways, the town of Nez Perce always kept changing, even though Ray and Fran wanted it to stay the same. They wanted to stay the same, because it was safe and predictable that way.

Mainly, what riled up a lot of locals was knowing that the Californians tried to buy up property right up against the river, where people would dock their boats and go fishing. According to Ray, it was bad enough that a fella couldn't fish anymore, then you'd have a mess of Californians telling you what you could or couldn't do about most anything. Ray harped and hollered about the "bastard Californians" most every night, and wished the river would sweep the "sons of bitches and their fancy homes into the fuckin' Pacific Ocean."

The eastern end of town was where whites first settled there. Some of these houses still stood. The better ones were kept up and fixed up for modern times. They were usually larger, two or three story Victorian homes, with nice paint, manicured lawns, and shade trees where folks could enjoy long, hot summer days. Already, leaves on the trees turned yellow, orange, and brown, which pleased tourists and photographers no end.

Nez Perce didn't even really get to become a town until 1909. At first, the town wasn't even called "Nez Perce." The early pioneers didn't call it much of anything, until long after Chief Joseph and his people were chased off the land. For some reason, the town was named in their honor. Statues and murals of Joseph and his tribe decorated the town, and drew in lots of tourists and sightseers from all over ... especially Californians.

A lot of the first white men here were of Irish, Welsh, or Scots descent. Aunt Fran always pointed out that it was the O'Malleys, the O'Fearnas, and even a few McDonalds, McQueens, and MacNaughtons who made homes along the banks of the Columbia River, after they ran the Native Americans off. Almost every name in town sounded Irish, Welsh, or Scottish, except for the Mexicans and the intruders from California. Ray often harped that only the Scots, Welsh, or Irish were dumb enough to settle in the deserts of northern Oregon.

One thing about it, though. Statues, paintings, and murals of Native Americans were better to look at than that of kilted bagpipers, leprechauns, and drunken bricklayers.

Once I got into town, I wandered past the post office, the library, a few gas stations, a diner or two, one marijuana dispensary, and even a couple of strip joints. There were a few churches in town, mainly the Mormons, Jehovah's Witnesses, Baptists, and Presbyterians. The *Ba-Hai* attempted to start one up there, back in the Eighties, but left because they were probably too weird. Most Catholics went to church in Hermiston, because it shared the same priest with the one in Nez Perce, and had more room for the Irish and Mexicans, than the dinky brick and concrete building which sat just a stone's throw from the riverbank.

I strolled along the narrow sidewalk, as thunder rumbled in the distance. Darkened storm clouds appeared from the north. I nearly cussed myself for walking, and wondered if I'd have to pester Uncle Ray or Aunt Fran for a ride home, later on. It was about two in the afternoon, and Mom was already on her way to the old folks' home in Hermiston. I hated burdening anyone, and hated to imagine what Ray or Fran said if I bugged them for a lift.

The Warriors Den sat next to the high school. It was built the same year the school opened, in 1967, and was a good place for kids. It had a jukebox with the latest hits, and a whole bunch of golden oldies.

In the past, the Warriors Den decorated itself to fit the tastes and times. It used to have a Fifties look, and for a short while was associated with the *Art Deco* thing. Some years back, it played homage to anything and everything *Star Wars*. It also went out of its way to favor the Mexican kids, and even had a separate menu for them.

The current owner really liked old movies, and had tons of black and white glossy photographs of stars from the olden days, such as Frank Sinatra, Marilyn Monroe, Audrey Hepburn, Katharine Hepburn, Bogey, James Cagney, the Duke, Clark Gable, Spencer Tracy, and Lauren Bacall.

This is where I'd have lunch with my soon-to-be-ex-boyfriend Danny O'Roarke.

I tended to show up everywhere early, and this was no exception. This being Saturday, there was a whole bunch of kids at the Warriors Den. Some smiled and said 'hi' when I got there. A few gave me a "so-what?" kind of look, while others gave me the evil eye.

I pretended to ignore the mean ones. Truth is, I wanted to rip off their heads and shit down their necks. Had I not been so small, wimpy, and shrimpy, I would've said nasty things to them, too. If I dared to retaliated against them, they might very well have ripped off my head and shit down my neck. I hated the horrible things these assholes said to me, and about me. But what else could I do but walk away, grin, and bear it?

I headed to a booth at the end of the diner, closest to the restrooms. Someone put a dollar or two in the jukebox. Seconds later, an old *Boston* tune, *More Than a Feeling,* played for all to enjoy or cuss about.

A few guys voiced their disapproval by hollering, "Turn off that old fogey shit!" while a sophomore girl claimed that her parents and grandparents listened to it, "so shut your ass up, asswipe!"

I only breathed a sigh of relief, glad it wasn't something real horrible like *Kenye West.*

"Gerry O'Fearna!" hollered Morgan Petrie, as she wandered to my table with silverware, a menu, and a glass of ice cold water. "What brings you out on a rainy day?"

"A date," I said, with an awkward grin.

"Danny?" whispered Morgan.

"You got it."

"Then it's a table for two," said Morgan, heading back into the kitch-en.

Morgan was a junior at the high school. Although she was a Californian, Morgan was still cool with me and Danny being an item. She was kind of fat, and not much younger than me, with a slightly pugged nose. She wasn't the prettiest girl around, but she was one of the nicest. If I ever had a rotten day, Morgan was always there with a kind word and a shoulder to lean on. Morgan was cool. She was *safe*.

I sat there alone in my booth, listening to the music and tapping my fingers nervously, waiting on Danny. I glanced at my *Timex,* then stupidly at a big *Coca-Cola clock* upon the wall. Danny was supposed to be there at two-thirty, and it was only a few minutes past two! I don't know why I was so anxious. I always got that way whenever Danny and me went out together. I don't know why. I always felt kind of inferior around Danny. I constantly wondered and worried how I got so lucky to have him as a companion, a partner, and a lover.

It was a few minutes later, when Danny O'Roarke finally got to the Warriors Den.

It was right about the same time when a *Mouth and MacNeil* song played their one-hit wonder from a million years ago, something titled *How Do You Do?* The restaurant erupted with a loud and angry, "What the fuck?", followed by an overall sense of hate and discontent.

At least this took the attention away from a couple of gay kids who were going to have lunch together.

4

"How's it going?" Danny asked me as he approached my booth, where I waited impatiently.

I smiled, glad that Danny finally showed up. I motioned to a seat opposite me across the table. My heart raced, both hands sweat, and I suddenly found it hard to speak. It was always like that whenever I got around Danny O'Roarke. I'd always get a stupid look on my face, then babble on like a complete fool.

Anyways, Danny wasn't a big guy, maybe only five-six. It still seemed like he kind of towered over me. Most guys towered over me! Anyways, although Danny wasn't the tallest tree in the forest, he was gorgeous. At least I thought so. He had shoulder-length, blonde hair, a narrow face, high cheekbones, and the most awesome and stunning green eyes! He also had a good tan. He was into jogging, and a cyclist. It wouldn't surprise me if he ran or biked ten miles, before getting dressed to see me.

Danny was eighteen, with a nice smile and an aura to match. He had just graduated from Nez Perce High in June, and was only days away from heading to college at *Portland State University*.

To my regret, I wouldn't get to see him on a regular basis.

Danny wore a long-sleeved, blue plaid shirt, a green, wool vest, a pair of brand new blue, denim shorts, cut just above the knees, and red *Converse*. He kept his legs shaved, because he said it held back the wind resistance when he jogged or rode bicycles.

I wanted Danny to lean over and plant a kiss on my cheek. Instead, he settled on a measly handshake. While Danny was slowly getting okay with being gay, he still didn't want most people to know it. Mainly, he wanted to keep it a secret.

Anyways, just about everyone in town already knew that Danny was gay, just like they knew I was and still am. Danny went out with girls for a while, thinking that way he'd hide the truth. He even went so far as to try fooling with one, and just couldn't get it up. The girl he tried to mess with claimed that he ran from the backseat of the car, fighting to get his pants back on, screeching and crying like a "faggot little bitch!" Guess that date ended badly.

Anyways, when Danny came out to a few friends around town, he might as well have announced it on a bullhorn. It was impossible to keep secrets in Nez Perce. Tell anybody anything you might as well tell the whole wide world, because within a day or two everybody will know about it, anyways.

Anyways, Danny thought that his relationship with me was a secret, and that we were just a couple of pals, hanging out "for shits and chuckles." In our case, shits and chuckles usually involved the two of us doing the nasty in the back of his van, and I hoped that day was no different. I knew that Danny was leaving town in just a few days, and then our dates would be few and far between. It scared me to think that Danny might find another guy up in Portland, break up with me, then leave me with a broken heart, sleepless nights, and a lot of tears.

In a way, I kind of had it easy, compared to Danny. My family already knew that I liked guys. While it sometimes led to weird questions or even a few snotty jabs from Uncle Ray, they never really condemned me for it much.

Neither Danny's mom or divorced dad were cool with him and me seeing each other. Just what was Danny doing, hanging out with a "fruit" like me?

Danny's mom wanted him to go through some kind of therapy, to help "straighten" him out. She was an angry old bitch who worked at a dollar store in Hermiston, and gave me the evil eye anytime I went in there. I'd just go in there to buy a measly *Shasta Cola* or a *U-No* bar, and she'd have to tell me that I was Hell bound for steering Danny the wrong way, or something. She figured that Danny suffered from a mental illness or perversion. She couldn't understand why Danny and me loved each other, and tried to write it off as a phase that'd pass, once Danny found the right girl. She refused to give me a "hello" or "have a nice day", no matter where we were at.

Even being in the same state with Joyce O'Roarke was horrible, and yet another reminder that some people refused to accept that guys like Danny or me even existed.

Danny's old man, Steve O'Roarke, was a truck driver from over in eastern Idaho. He had just got remarried, and had a new wife and step-kids in Burley. He rarely saw Danny, never invited him to meet the new family, and threatened to pound the snot out of his kid for "turning queer." He planned on giving Danny a knuckle sandwich one of these days.

Danny avoided seeing Steve whenever he hauled goods along I-84 or along 395, which he often did. I didn't even know what Steve looked like. Nor did I want to. I didn't want anything bad happening to Danny, should he and Steve's path crossed, which eventually it just might.

"You order yet?" asked Danny, as he sat down across the table from me in the booth.

"Not yet," I answered. "I been waiting on you."

Danny gave me a warm smile. "So, how's the artwork coming?"

"Aw, not too bad. Right now I'm working on a dragon."

"Bring it with you?"

"Uh... Not today," I said, with a shrug. "Thought about it, but it passed my mind."

"Oh, c'mon Gerry!" Danny glared at me, like I was HIV-positive or something. "I love your art! I meant what I said earlier.... What I always told you. When I become a big-time author, I want you to do my book covers for me!"

Before I got another word in, Danny kept on me. "I think you're really talented, Ger. So do a lotta other people. Damn it! You can go places with your art, if only you had the balls to show it off. How the hell do you expect to go anywhere, if you don't brag on yourself a little? Or a lot?"

Anger surged through me. I nearly lashed out at Danny. It wasn't because he was wrong. In truth, I hoped he was right. I simply didn't want to admit it. I knew I had to take my art more serious. Danny knew it, Old Lady Goodwin knew it. Mom knew it. I sorta knew it. I needed to display my drawings and pastels, show them off, learn to take praise graciously and criticism constructively. Some people believed in me, even when I didn't always believe in myself. I had to really work at it, each and every day, like a ritual or a routine. I sometimes knew I could do better, even though I often feared that my stuff was "too long haired, wild-assed, and not worth a shit", like what Uncle Ray said.

I sometimes laid awake at night, thinking I'd never be worth a shit, either as an artist or even as a person. I let doubt and anxiety get the better of me. Danny's comments were just a reminder of a reality which I tried to avoid, and never would.

"You can pout all you want," said Danny. "But it don't change a thing. You gotta get yourself out there! Hell, if you don't, you'll regret it for the rest of your life!"

I sighed. I felt like my insides were all tied in knots. But instead of making me feel better, Danny made me feel worse! Somehow, he made me feel lousy and inferior. Not only did I feel inferior to Danny O'Roarke, the fear of losing him was more horrible than I could imagine!

I knew that Danny wanted out of Nez Perce, out of eastern Oregon, and make something of himself. He wanted to be a writer, and wasn't half-bad at it. He had earned a few scholarships for his writing, and I just knew that he'd find himself on the bestsellers' list.

While Danny sought fame and fortune, I'd live in poverty and unforgiving obscurity. Danny's talents amounted to something. My artwork wasn't worth a shit, and probably never would be.

I didn't want Danny heading off to Portland. Not only was he a good-looking guy, he was *hot!* I mean, sweet and *hot!* His mere presence gave me a hard-on. Whether he blew it with a girl or not, Danny never let me down, when it came to the nasty. At the time, he was the only guy to get me in the sack. I'll always remember the night I lost my virginity to him, a year before, and it was magic! I hoped we'd end up dropping pants later that day, and I couldn't wait! My first time was his first time, too. I wanted Danny as my very own, and stay with me a little longer. I dreaded thoughts of him leaving in a few days!

My hopes for Danny's career collided with desires of keeping him around, even if staying in Nez Perce made him miserable and unhappy. Was I being selfish? Yes! Did I care? Hell, no! I didn't want to let Danny go, and didn't know where I'd be, without him in my life.

Holy cow. Danny was *hot!* I just knew he'd find another guy, when he got to Portland. Then I'd be alone, with no prospects or no meaning in my own existence. I'd stay in Nez Perce for the rest of my life, and never be worth a shit.

Danny reached out and caressed my hand. It felt good. It made me believe, and want to believe, that he truly cared for me, and that he cared for my dreams of becoming an artist . . . a *real* artist!

Seconds later, Danny pulled his hand away, realizing that others might be watching us. He feared that others in the Warriors Den was judging us, evaluating us... thinking, suspecting, or even knowing that we were more than just friends. Danny wanted to uphold the façade that we were just chums, and nothing more.

But, hell, everybody in the Warriors Den already knew better.

Danny sucked in a deep breath. "I love you, Gerry," he whispered, hoping no one else heard him. "I only want you to be happy. For both of us to be happy!"

"I love you, too," I answered, fighting back tears.

"It's just that..." Danny rolled his eyes back, and bit his bottom lip. "Shit, Gerry. The only thing I wanted was to get out of this town, and go someplace where my writing will find a decent audience! That's how I feel about your art! I mean.... Damn it, you're good! I want people to know that! But they won't know it if you keep it hidden away in your fucking bedroom! I mean...." Danny stopped. "I mean.... Oh, hell! I meant what I said. I don't want to be just a writer. I want to be the best writer that ever came out of Oregon, better than Ursula K. Le Guin or fucking Ken Kesey! I want to be the best damned writer in the whole wide world! And I want the best covers on them!"

"I know that," I mumbled, as someone had the nerve to put a Kenye West song on the jukebox.

"I don't want to trust just any artist to work on the covers of my books," said Danny. "Or just anybody looking to make a quick buck."

Danny looked me straight in the eye. "I want you to be the artist who can motivate readers to pick up my books, check them out, then place their hard-earned money on the counter, and buy what I put my heart and soul into! I want you to be the artist who can do that for me!"

I looked away from Danny. Though I tried holding them back, a few teardrops dripped from my eyes. I felt like a pathetic, sorry-ass, won't-be-worth-a-shit wimp, who whines and cries about everything! I couldn't help myself! Danny's comment hit me where it counted! I couldn't speak. I picked up the napkin from the table, and tried to wipe away the emotions which refused to be held back.

"Ready to order?" Morgan Petrie asked, as she approached the table with a warm smile and a pitcher of water. "Need more time?"

"I'm ready," said Danny. "I'll take a .... Warrior Burger and a large *Coke*, please."

"Fries, salad, or tots?" asked Morgan, jotting Danny's order down.

"Salad, please," said Danny.

"And you, Gerry?" Morgan let out a funny little giggle at my moistened, red eyes and sad puppy dog look.

"The same," I mumbled, pasting on an idiotic grin while pretending that I was all right.

"Fries, tater tots, or salad?"

"Fries," I said. "I guess."

"You *guess?*" snickered Morgan.

"Yeah," I said, nervously. "Fries.... *Fries!* Fries'll do."

"Then fries it'll be." Morgan jotted down my order. "And a large Coke?"

My throat tightened. Unable to say anything, I simply nodded.

"Coming right up!" said Morgan, heading back to the kitchen.

"I meant what I said," whispered Danny, as he also got a bit teary-eyed. "I think you're good, Gerry. Real good. And I want others to see how good you are, too. Please.... *Please....* For me. Take your art a lot more serious, and have the balls to show the world that you're an awesome fucking artist. Okay? *Okay?*"

"Okay," I answered, my voice barely heard over the racket of loud conversation and music blaring, from the jukebox. Daring to take Danny's hand in mine, I managed somehow to smile. "I promise I will... I promise! I'll do it, Danny.... I *promise!*"

5

A few minutes later, Morgan brought Danny and me our orders. We ate quietly, making occasional small talk and stuff. The music on the juke-box went from the modern sounds and a few nice tunes from our grand-parents' time. Morgan refilled our water glasses, while we listened to an old *Culture Club* song, *Karma Chameleon*. A few guys griped, groaned, harped, moaned and mumbled about "that faggot Boy George shit!"

We finished lunch, and paid for it at the counter. Danny slapped me on the back, and asked, "Now what do you wanna do?"

"I dunno," I said, shrugging.

"Wanna go to the park?" asked Danny.

I glanced outside, hoping there was no chance of rain in the next hour or so. "Sure," I agreed. "Why not?"

Even if it wasn't raining at the time, the wind blew like an old whore, as Uncle Ray would say. A breeze swept in from the ocean, and snaked along the Columbia. It was damp, and chilled clear to the bone.

Danny and I sprinted to his ancient, green *Chevy* van, parked out at the far end of the lot. We hopped in, where it was a little warmer.

Danny's van was an old beater that had who-knows-how many owners over the years. It had the dents, bumps, bashes, gashes, cracks and bruises to prove it. Danny got it for a steal, from a guy who needed cash to pay for alcohol and drug rehab classes. I'm guessing the van was already thirty years old or more when Danny bought it. The back seats were gone, and replaced by camping gear and a ragged, twin mattress. The front bucket seats were torn up, real bad. They'd been patched together with tons of duct tape, and leaked upholstery everywhere. Most of the gauges on the dashboard no longer worked very good.

The Chevy roared to life, once Danny finally got it started. It bellowed smoke like an old Republican, and spewed black fumes from the exhaust pipe.

Now that nobody was watching, Danny leaned over, threw an arm around my shoulder, and kissed me on the cheek. "I love you," he said, with a smile that absolutely melted my heart.

"I love you, too," I said, as our lips met in a warm, wet smooch.

Danny revved up the Chevy, put it in *DRIVE,* and then we headed out onto 395 towards Hermiston, to a favorite spot near Eleventh Street.

The traffic was hectic, chaotic, and crazy. Then again, I always figured that any traffic was a nightmare. Anyways, I never liked cars, dealing with other cars, or driving. What the hell do I know?

"I hear that Wal-Mart is hiring," said Danny, as he turned off of 395 onto Elm Street, then headed onto Eleventh.

"Okay," I said, in a "so what?" manner.

"Ever think about getting a job there?" Danny glared at me.

"Not really."

"Ever think about getting a job, at all?" pressed Danny, like an old man scolding his spoiled kid.

"I already work for my Uncle Ray," I said, unable to hide my animosity.

"You *live* with your Uncle Ray." Danny smiled, maliciously. "You ought to be working for him, Gerry, while you're living under his roof. You ever think about getting a *real* job? You know, where you make *real* money?"

My fists hardened, as my face got red with frustration. I knew where this was going... where it always went. Danny always harassed me about getting a job, or to go out and earn some extra cash. Not only did it make me mad. It added to my sense of inferiority. "Can we just not talk about it?" I snapped.

Danny sighed, in a way which told me that he had more ammunition to fire at me. He wouldn't use it... at least not at the moment.

We stopped at a railroad crossing, as a *Union Pacific* train flew past us. Not a word was spoken as we sat there, waiting to continue on. The mood inside the van was tense.

Finally, we turned a corner at *Good Shepherd Medical Center,* on our way to *Victory Square,* next to Orchard Street.

This was a part of town that Uncle Ray called "Spanish Hermiston", because many of the people living there were Mexican. Ray sure couldn't carry a tune any better than I can. But he'd try to sing an old Ben E. King song known as *Spanish Harlem,* and just replace the word "Harlem" with "Hermiston."

I liked Ben E. King's version a lot better.

Danny stopped, and shut off the engine. The van was so noisy, you couldn't think. The sounds of silence were like a sunny day. I took a deep breath, let it go slowly, and stared through the dusty windshield. A steady stream of cars streamed through the neighborhood, which had its share of restaurants, gas stations, and a few indie car lots. The skies were gray with thick clouds, as a heavy breeze shook leaves from the trees.

I looked over at Danny. He kind of stared blankly, off into space. He wore a sort of sad look on his face, like he was forced into some hard decisions, with no easy answers.

I reached over to take Danny's hand into mine. Mustering my courage, I asked the one question I dreaded an answer to. "So.... Uhm.... Danny .... What day do you leave? .... For college?"

"Tuesday," said Danny, like he also dreaded it.

"This *coming* Tuesday?"

"This coming Tuesday. Gotta go through orientation, buy my books, get moved into the dorms." Danny sighed. "Pulling out in just a few days."

"Wish you didn't have to go." I squeezed Danny's hand, as tight as I could.

"What the fuck choice do I have?" hollered Danny. "I mean... goddamn.... I gotta get on with my life, don't I? And I sure as hell can't do that, working at some lousy dead-end job around here."

I was shocked at Danny's sudden outburst. "Look, Dan, I didn't mean...."

"I gotta make something of myself!" interrupted Danny. "I sure as shit won't do it in Nez Perce. That might be okay for you, hanging around and not getting anywhere, but not me!"

I shook my head, and sighed. It seemed that all Danny and I did now was fight. It wasn't always like that, but now it seemed like our relationship was coming apart. It made me miserable as hell. I couldn't imagine life without Danny O'Roarke, and yet that reality showed itself before my very eyes. "Sorry," I apologized, sounding like a moron. My heart raced, as sweat rolled down my back. "I didn't mean..."

"Look, Gerry," Danny cut in. "I'm not sure if I wanna leave Nez Perce. Truth is, I'm kind of scared. *Jesus!* I'm moving to fucking *Portland!* I was always taught to hate that big-ass, fucking city, and here I am about to move there!" Danny chuckled. "I mean, who in the hell from eastern Oregon likes Portland?"

"You oughta hear what Ray and Fran says about it."

Danny cupped my hand in his. With that, we again locked lips, and kissed for nearly a minute.

Right about then, two young Mexican boys strolled by the van, and voiced their disapproval by mumbling, *"Los homosexuales,"* along with a few unflattering comments in Spanish.

Embarrassed and humiliated, Danny tried to pull away. Already, we were too far along in the mood for love to stop now. I refused to halt this magic moment. I ran my fingers through Danny's blonde hair, as my other hand caressed his knee.

I sneaked my hand into Danny's short blue jeans, where I delicately massaged his thigh. Danny gave me a one-arm hug around the shoulders, as he reached into my pants to arouse me more than I already was. My heart beat out of control, as my body heat soared by leaps and bounds.

Danny nibbled on my earlobe, as the emotions nearly proved too great. Happiness and joy took the place of fear and sorrow. I rested my head on Danny's shoulder, as the tears dripped from my eyes. No matter what the next few days may have brought, Danny was mine, and I was his. He felt so warm and gentle in my arms. The whole wide world might have judged us, but it didn't matter. We were in love, and that was the only thing that counted.

Danny revved up the Chevy's roaring engine, which startled the geese and seagulls hanging around the park. Most scattered in flight. Danny and I rushed to a nearby hideout, where we'd get needed privacy.

We got back onto Eleventh Street, headed east on Elm, crossed 395 next to Wal-Mart, then zipped through Hermiston. After passing a fair number of homes and small businesses, we got onto the Diagonal Road, and sped out of town.

We soon made a right and meandered down a long, winding gravel road, where no one lived.

About a mile or two later, we reached an old, empty farmhouse at a dead-end. There was nothing out there but a small herd of cattle, munching on tall grass and alfalfa. Here, we'd be alone.

Danny stopped at a wide spot at the dead end, under the shade of an apple tree. Neither of us said much, knowing already what was coming up. We'd been down that path before. As thunder rumbled in the distance, rain splattered upon the windshield.

Danny smiled as I beat him to the back of the van. I made myself comfortable on the mattress, and eagerly peeled off my shoes. Then, without a second thought, I quickly slipped out of my shorts and underwear, then tossed them carelessly by the back doors. Cool, damp air drifted in from outside, across my bare legs, crotch, and backside.

While I caressed my balls, Danny joined me on the mattress. I threw my arms around his waist and showered him with kisses.

Danny gently lied me on my back, as he ran his fingers through my hair. One of his hands reached down to pleasure me. I unzipped his pants to do the same for him. Although the inside of the van was a bit musty and cold, my need and hunger for Danny warmed me.

Danny worked out of his Levi shorts. I pressed both hands to his bare butt. Our legs tied together, as we embraced.

After a few minutes of foreplay, mostly hugging, kissing, cuddling, and a few minutes of *sixty-nine,* I wrapped my arms around the back of the passenger side bucket seat, and positioned myself for what came next. I spread my legs in anticipation of my favorite hobby.

Danny slipped on a *Trojan,* which he kept in a tackle box next to some fishing gear. Slowly, he knelt behind and guided himself into me.

It always kind of hurt right at first, and I let out with a loud, low moan. My fingers dug into the bucket seat, my teeth clenched, and sweat poured from my face and forehead. My knuckles were a bone-white, as air rushed from my lungs.

"You okay?" asked Danny, clutching my upper thighs and hips.

"I'm a'right," I gasped, in a whisper.

Gradually, the pain subsided. I gave Danny a labored grin, then kissed him on the cheek.

As Danny thrusted himself into me, rain beat down on the Chevy in a heavy downpour. My left arm held tightly to the bucket seat, as my right cupped my balls and penis. I closed both eyes and savored Danny's rhythmic movements on me, and *in* me. The van rocked back and forth, wildly.

It would be obvious to any onlooker that, whatever Danny and me were doing in there, it wasn't knitting.

"Oh, God!" Danny cried out, his breathing swift and shallow. He reached under my hoody and tee-shirt, to rub my chest and tummy. He planted a number of wet kisses to the back of my neck. I opened my mouth to remind him that, once more, I loved him.

What came out of my mouth was an involuntary, high-pitched shriek.

I'm a screamer...

"Stop it, Gerry!" snickered Danny. "You're making me laugh, you motherfucker!"

I didn't scream because it hurt. I screamed because it felt so good ... and because I just couldn't help it. The longer Danny went on, the louder and longer I squalled, until Danny started giggling hysterically.

"You okay?" he asked, pulling out as he caught his breath.

"Why'd you stop?" I hollered, collapsing onto the mattress. "Don't stop now! Keep going, Dan! *Please!* Just keep going!"

"Holy shit," whispered Danny, tiredly, cradling me in his arms. "You made it sound like I was in here skinning a cat!"

My heart beat out of control as I hugged Danny.

"You okay, Gerry?" Danny rubbed my shoulders, and kissed me on the lips. "Wanna go on?"

"Sure," I said, fingering the crack of my butt as I gave myself a hand job.

"Get on your back, and I'll do you like a missionary."

I did what I was told. I placed a feather pillow to my head, and spread my legs eagle in anticipation.

"Ready?" asked Danny.

I nodded 'yes,' and smiled eagerly.

"As long as you promise not to howl like you did the last time," said Danny, kneeling above me.

I gave Danny a hug, while I wrapped my legs around his waist.

With a nervous smile, Danny got on top of me. I bit my bottom lip, clenched my fists, and closed both eyes.

Once more, a groan crept from my mouth, as Danny entered inside me. "I'm not hurting you?" he asked, anxiously. "Am I?"

"No!" I hollered, as tears dripped from my eyes. "Just fuckin' get on with it.... *Please?... Danny... Please!...*"

Our lips met in a kiss.

I hugged Danny with all my might. My legs locked around him, at the ankles. Danny started banging me, slow at first, then later with a speed and ferocity which I never once felt from him, before.

"Not so fast!" I begged, wondering if my wide eyes were about to pop out of their sockets, at any moment.

"Sorry," apologized Danny, in a heartfelt whine. "I didn't realize..."

"Please!... Just make it last ... as long as you can...."

Danny obeyed me. He was more interested me making me happy, than in pleasuring himself.

As my fingers toyed with Danny's long, blonde hair, others grasped onto his shirt and wool vest. "I love you," I moaned. I dug my fingers into the vest so hard, I nearly ripped a hole through it.

"I love you, too," responded Danny, while steadily pumping on me.

"Oh god, oh fuck!" I let out, opening my eyes to stare upon the roof of Danny's ratty old van. "Oh Jesus, my *God!* Feels so good.... Feels so *good!"*

"Yeah," agreed Danny. "To me, too!"

"Fuck me, Dan!" I screamed, as loud as I could. "Oh god, man! Fuck me, Dan! Please fuck *me!"*

"What do ya think I'm doing, Gerry? I *am* fucking you! What the hell do you think I'm *doing*?"

"Whatever it is you're doing, don't stop!" I cried, as the sounds of rain echoed throughout the van.

I rested my head onto the pillow, and imagined myself in a field of soft grass, surrounded by flowers and trees. Bright rays of sunlight blessed Danny and me with a gentle warmth. Birds sang of my love, need, and affection for Danny O'Roarke. Had God allowed it, I could've made love to him, from now to the end of time. I never wanted this moment to end. Nothing else mattered in the world. I begged for Danny to stay with me, as I lived and died and found myself reborn in his arms.

Paradise lost, and Heaven is destroyed by a cruel, merciless foe....

"I'm gonna come!" I hollered, anxiously lifting my hoody and shirt up. I screamed loud enough to break the eardrums of anyone close enough to hear it.

Semen spurted out, onto my legs, hips, and hoody.

Danny pulled out of me, swiftly removed the condom, and jacked off until he also reached climax. He dropped next to me on the mattress, as we embraced as only lovers could.

"Danny," I said, rubbing his face softly. By now, the emotions had gotten the best of me, as tears ran freely from my eyes. "Don't leave me! Please don't leave me! Whatever you do, Danny O'Roarke, don't you dare leave me! Stay with me, forever! Please, Danny, I beg you! Don't ever leave me!"

"I.... I promise," said Danny. Holding me tightly in his arms, he kissed me upon the forehead. "Trust me, Gerry.... I... I promise never to leave you. I promise never to let you go...."

"Promise?" I wept, as some of my tears dripped upon Danny's shoulder and soaked into his plaid shirt.

"Yeah," assured Danny, caressing my hair and dampened face. "You have my word, Gerry. I'll never let you go! I *promise!* I promise never let you go! ...."

6

Danny and I got on our shorts and shoes, then headed back into Nez Perce. A few minutes later, we got to Danny's house to shower and clean up.

Danny lived in a large, two-story house. It was one of the first homes built in town, soon after whites began taking over. It was built by Danny's great-great-grandparents or uncles or something, and had withstood the test of time. It had added new rooms, indoor plumbing, electricity, oil heat, and other stuff.

Who knows how many O'Roarkes had lived in that old house, over the years?

Because it was so big, the O'Roarke home was a place where other family members would "camp out", and stay for a long visit, from a job loss or other hardships of one kind or another. Kind of like me and Mom staying at Uncle Ray and Aunt Fran's house. That is, until we got back on our feet.

Danny always griped and harped and complained because him and his mom had to deal with some lazy jerks living in the basement, who promised to get out when they got back on their feet, kind of like Mom and me. Somehow, those staying at the O'Roarke's never got back on their feet, until someone else had to put their feet down, and insist they get back on their feet.

Danny and I blundered into the living room, where his mom sat there watching some goofy-assed romance movie on *Netflix*. She watched TV with one eye and gossiped with her sister on the phone with the other. She just got done giggling and telling lies about someone or another, when Danny and me showed up.

Danny's mom, Joyce O'Roarke, sort of smiled at him, until she saw me walk through the door. She gave us both the evil eye, then told the person she was talking to she'd call them back.

Danny already knew he was on the shit-list with Dear Old Mom, or Our Beloved Leader, or Ernst Blofeld, or other names he called her. He motioned for me to head upstairs to his bedroom, while he prepared himself for The Talk.

I ran upstairs, feeling kind of bad for leaving Danny to confront that horrible woman. But I tend to avoid conflict like the plague. When it comes to mean-looks, and even meaner words, I'm a real coward.

I got to Danny's room, just as the lecture started. I got a sick feeling in my stomach, and wondered if this awkward moment would lead to my walking papers, and expulsion from the House of O'Roarke. Well, I never liked Joyce O'Roarke, and she never liked me. She never approved of Danny's relationship with me, and never believed that her beautiful, tow-headed child was THAT WAY. I guess it was one thing if I was and still am THAT WAY. She didn't care what I did with myself, as long as it didn't involve Danny. She probably thought I spent my free time prancing around the woods in frizzy shirts, tights, pointy hats, pointy shoes, pointy ears and pointy wings, spreading fairy dust on all the happy little critters and pretty little flowers.

Guess it was okay for boys in the O'Fearna clan to like other boys.

But, by God, no O'Roarke male was gonna turn out THAT WAY!

Joyce O'Roarke won't have it!

Once I blundered into the bedroom, my soon-to-be-ex-boyfriend was getting his butt chewed by Dear Old Mom. It made me sick, sad, angry, and hurt. I wanted to stick up for Danny, but my cowardice kept me from it. I wanted nothing more than to get in the shower with him, so we'd take turns cleaning each other off. I debated on stripping off my clothes, then wait for Danny to get over his nightly browbeating from Fearless Leader. Thoughts of getting thrown out on my ass kept me from feeling at ease or comfortable. I took a deep breath and awaited the outcome.

I overheard two sets of screaming matches taking place in the house. One was between Danny and the Queen Mother. The second took place between other members of the O'Roarke clan, those who somehow couldn't get back on their feet.

Quentin O'Roarke, his wife Daisy, and their kids had moved into the basement, and had an absolutely terrible time getting back on their feet. Much of this was brought on by Quentin's lousy attitude and opinions on most everything. This usually led to his getting canned off a large assortment of jobs, from construction to carpentry to pumping gas or selling lumber or tater chips or pop at the *7 Eleven*. Quentin wasn't afraid to tell his employers, who naturally wasn't as smart as he was, to fuck off, to go fuck themselves, or simply "fuck you."

Moments later, Quentin would be handed a paycheck, then ordered to fuck off, fuck himself, or "fuck you."

Quentin might get an odd-job here and there. As a rule, these opportunities always ended the same way.

Badly.

Anyways, Quentin now spent most days watching dumb action films and sex comedies on Netflix, harping on what "that dumb nigger Obama" was doing to the country, and bitching about the lack of jobs in Nez Perce, thanks to all the Spicks who took them from white people.

Right about then, Quentin and Daisy's seventeen-year-old daughter Eileen was kind of sweet on a kid named Luis Ortega. Luis was nineteen, and worked as a mechanic for his uncle who ran a *Sinclair* station on Eleventh Street in Hermiston. I kind of liked Eileen. She was also a senior at the high school, and was cool with the idea me dating her cousin Danny.

Anyways, Eileen planned on meeting Luis at the Warriors Den, and Quentin would have none of it. He hated seeing his kid hanging out with some "greasy, good-for-nothing beaner." He thought she'd get knocked up, then be stuck with some ugly half-breed child to take care of.

I sort of kind of knew Luis Ortega. He was nice enough, never made waves, stayed polite, and smiled an awful lot. I also thought he was kind of cute. Too bad he was straight, or I would've been far more interested.

I heard Quentin and Eileen telling each other to go fuck off, fuck themselves, and "fuck you!" Finally, a door leading into the basement from outside creaked open, then slammed shut. I heard Eileen tell Quentin to go eat shit and die, then accused him of fucking his mother. Then I heard Quentin and Daisy refer to Eileen as a slut and a whore, while ordering her to get her ass back in the house, or telling her to move the fuck out and don't fucking come back, "you sorry, ungrateful little twat!"

A car door opened, when slammed shut with a loud *BAM!* Then a small sports car sped off in the night.

The basement door then slammed, as Quentin and Daisy began telling each other to fuck off, fuck themselves, and "fuck you."

Seconds later, Danny wandered into his bedroom, wearing a whipped puppy dog look which melted my heart. Without giving it a second thought, I gave him a tight squeeze around the hips, then sneaked a gentle little peck on his cheek.

Danny returned the kiss, with a smooch on the forehead. His eyes were red and moist, from tears. His teeth gritted in rage. "Fucking bitch," he whispered. Tiredly, he sat down on his single bed in the corner, and slipped off his shoes and socks.

About that same time, the Queen Mother got in her *Toyota Tercel*, zipped out of the driveway, then rushed off, the engine buzzing in the rain and darkness.

"Where's she going?" I asked, like a blithering moron.

"Who the hell cares?" groaned Danny, tossing his vest to the floor as he unbuttoned his shirt and threw it, carelessly, upon the bed. "C'mon, let's go take a shower."

I undressed, placed my clothes in a pile against one wall, then followed Danny into a teensy little private bathroom, next to his bedroom.

Danny got the shower all nice and warm. The both of us hopped in, and pressed our nude bodies together in a loving embrace.

This wasn't quite as good as making love to Danny in the van earlier, but it was a darned close second. As we threw our arms around each other, our lips locked in a long, wet smooch. Cascades of water blessed us in a secular baptism.

I rested my head to Danny's shoulder, and we cuddled. Water dripped from our hair and body. Our hands and fingers were explorers, trekking across our lovers. I kissed Danny's neck and chest, while he rubbed my shoulders, my back, my hips, and my backside, and held onto me, close.

Knowing that we'd soon part tore at my very soul. I hoped and prayed that Danny would change his mind about moving to Portland. Silently, I begged him to stay in Nez Perce for another year, until I graduated high school. Then we'd start a new life together.

Still, it was wrong to hold Danny back. He had his own dreams and ambitions. Nez Perce was home, but it was also a dead-end. It prevented Danny from fulfilling his potential as a writer.

Selfish or not, I didn't care! A year wasn't that long! Was it? We'd be a year older, a year wiser, a bit more mature. Maybe he'd be a better writer by then. The main thing is, we'd still be a couple! That's all that mattered! I didn't care if I was being selfish, or not. Spending time with Danny, sharing meals, taking showers together, or screwing .... It was all paradise to me!

"I love you, Dan," I said, as streams of water caressed me.

"I love you, too," said Danny, tears mixing with the water which dripped down his handsome young face. He kissed me on the cheek. "I never loved anyone as much as I love you."

A sob escaped from my quivering lips. The emotions were too great of a burden. I struggled to hold them back, but couldn't. I started crying like a wimpy-assed baby. I just couldn't help it! What good is being strong, when you feel your whole life slipping away from you? Danny was my life! Nothing else mattered as much as him!

And yet, Danny O'Roarke was leaving for college in just a few days!

And there wasn't a damn thing I could do to stop him!

"Fuckin' goddamn Spicks in this shithole of a fuckin' goddamn town!" someone hollered from the basement. "Oughta line all them beaners up against a wall and shoot 'em, along with that nigger president we got!"

"Quentin," sighed Danny, rolling his eyes back. He was both frustrated and amused by the racket downstairs. "Never a dull moment with him around."

"Gimme half a chance," Quentin continued, "I'll kill Luis Fuckin' Ortega along with all them other wetback bastards!"

Although my sadness and sorrow was apparent, Quentin's outbursts threw me back into a cruel, harsh reality, which ruined this special moment!

I glanced at Danny. Tears blurred my vision.

Danny shut the water off. Suddenly, the bathroom got cold, damp, and dewy. A breeze drifted in from outside. Like most old houses in town, the O'Roarke residence was a wind tunnel, especially when cold air blew in from the river. It chilled the mind, body, soul, and spirit.

Danny and I stepped out of the shower, and quickly dried ourselves off. Quentin and Daisy went on with their loud, potty-mouthed, drunken rants. Danny figured he needed to go downstairs, to keep them from knocking holes through the sheetrock walls in the basement, or breaking things.

Danny and I got dressed, then carefully headed downstairs to stop the commotion. The living room was empty, though the lights were left on, along with the huge, flat-screen TV. A hemorrhoid commercial was on, followed by an ad for life insurance. Danny glanced at me, nervously, as we both went to the site of a warzone.

I shook my head. The last thing I wanted was to get mixed up in a family squabble. I still had the twenty my Uncle Ray gave me that morning, and wanted to blow it at the Warriors Den or someplace else in town. I was kind of scared of Quentin and Daisy, and didn't pretend not to be. I wanted to leave that house, and hoped Danny felt the same.

"C'mon," urged Danny, taking my arm as we went downstairs, where a House of Horrors awaited us.

We found Daisy sitting at a flimsy, dining table, in the center of the basement's living room. She was a gal of thirty-five who used to be a high school beauty. Now, she got kind of ugly and fat. Her once smooth face and bright green eyes were wrinkled, creased, and dimmed from constant fear and worry, along with plenty of cigarettes and booze.

Quentin paced back and forth, along the cement floor of the dark, cluttered basement. When he was my age, Quentin was one of the best-looking guys around. Back then, he probably thought his future would be filled with hope and opportunity. Now, he was stuck living in a family member's house, eating on their dime, lost in anger, resentment, self-doubts, and an unhappy marriage. He was almost forty. His muscular body got bloated and flabby. His black hair was going grey, and flat stomach gave way to a beer belly. His eyes and jaw drooped, and he had a double chin. His white tee-shirt was covered with food stains, and soaked in sweat. He wore black sweat pants over his big butt and pale legs. He had a cigarette in one hand, and a bottle of *Henry Weinhard's Pale Ale* in the other.

The basement was a dump. There wasn't much furniture. Quentin, Daisy, and their three kids either slept on a hideaway bed, or on the floor. Dirty clothes scattered the floor. The place smelled like rotting food and dogshit. An overwhelming sense of defeat ruled over the basement. Seemed that Quentin threw his arms in the air and flat gave up. It was easier to blame his problems on other people, mainly "Spicks, Commies from Eugene and Portland, and that Commie nigger president".

"Quentin," said Danny, as we entered that filthy, stinking basement. "Daisy..."

Daisy hastily ran from the table to a tiny bathroom in one corner, probably to hide her shame and embarrassment.

Quentin gave Danny and me a quick looking over. Carelessly, he dropped some ashes on the floor, then took a swig of beer. "Well, Dan," he said, with an ornery grin. "Don't look to me like ya cornholed 'em too bad. Ain't walkin' around bowlegged or nothin'."

Whether Quentin's comments bothered Danny or not, he never said so. I wanted to come back with something twice as nasty or filthy, but didn't want a fist sandwich out of the deal. I pretended like his words didn't bother me, even though they did and still do.

Danny looked at me, then back over at Quentin. "So..." he said, hesitantly. "What's up?"

"Aw, hell," mumbled Quentin, sitting at the dining table. "Fuckin' Eileen, cattin' after that asshole Spick again."

Danny also sat down at the table. He urged me too, as well, but I didn't want to.

Quentin took a drag from his smoke. "Aw, Eileen started hangin' around with some dark-skinned, Don Juan, Spicky-Gonzalez type."

"Who?" asked Danny.

"Some filthy beaner who works for his uncle in one of them gas stations in Hermiston," said Quentin. "Luis.... Luigi...."

"Luis Ortega," I said.

"Yeah, that's it!" hollered Quentin. "Luis Fuckin' Ortega!"

Danny looked at me, then back over at Quentin.

"Wanna beer?" asked Quentin, motioning over at a small fridge in one corner of the basement. "Get yerselves a cold *Henry's*..." Quentin smirked. "'Less yer too good to drink with the straight folks...."

"I'll take one," said Danny, running over to fetch a beer. "What about you, Gerry?"

"I would," I said, reluctantly. "But Mom and Aunt Fran will shit a brick...."

"Fuck 'em!" roared Quentin. "Yer boyfriend ain't gonna say nothin', and neither in the fuck will me. Get yerself a goddamn cold one, and sit the fuck down, before I knock you down. Sit yer ass down here, O'Fearna. Makin' me nervous standin' there like that. I don't give a shit what you and Dan do together. You fuck him, he fucks you. You suck him, he sucks you. I don't give a fuck. I don't bite too bad. Rather drink with a white Irish faggot than a straight Spick or nigger, any day! Sit the fuck down, and hear what I gotta say..."

I did what Quentin told me to do. I didn't want to, but I did. Anyways, I sat down because it was better than getting knocked down.

Danny grabbed a beer for himself and me.

"Eileen thinks she oughta cat around with this fuckin' Luis and his asshole Spick family," said Quentin. "Eatin' tacos, drinkin' tequila, probably takin' turns with them brown-hided, horny illegal bastards, ridin' Catholic Spick cock."

Danny let out a chuckle, not because it was so funny, but because it was so *Quentin*.

"I don't give a fuck what she does," Quentin continued, "long as it ain't with a redskin or a Spick or a nigger. Far as I'm concerned, Spicks are worse than niggers, and the niggers are bad enough. Last time me and Daisy went on a road trip together, the car broke down somewhere in east Kansas, not too far from Topeka. Had to leave the car, catch a goddamn bus into Denver. Fuckin' bus was filled with jig-a-boos, screechin' and howlin' and laughin' and carryin' on like a buncha fuckin' savages, chasin' Tarzan through the jungle."

I wanted to leave, right then and there. For some idiotic reason, Danny wanted me to stay right there. Anyways, it was raining bad outside, so I was stuck.

"We got in that bus, which was crawlin' with a buncha loudmouth coons," said Quentin. "Couldn't get away from them screechin' hyenas, soon enough. Daisy couldn't fuckin' take it. Thought she'd have a nervous breakdown, or some goddamn thing. Worse thing about it, there was this old sow porch monkey and her black-assed little nigglette, suckin' on a big black titty, screechin' louder'n a fuckin' banshee."

"What's that gotta do with Eileen?" I asked, unable to hold back my anger.

"What the fuck does that gotta do with Eileen?" snapped Quentin, looking me straight in the eye. He could tell I was getting fed-up and tired. He didn't like it, and wanted me to know it. "I gotta get Eileen the fuck away from them greasy wetback bastards, and I thought.... I *hoped*.... You two faggots might wanna help me."

Had I not been such a wussy or a coward, I might have put Quentin in his place, or I would've done something stupid, so he'd put me in my place. But somehow, I found myself rooting for Eileen and Luis, and hoped they'd both run off and live happily ever after in a mansion, high above in the hills, and not in some trashy trailer park, with a car that won't start, along with noisy, meth-head neighbors. They'd never find peace or contentment, not with guys like Quentin around. Eileen and Luis would have to get as far away from Nez Perce as they possibly could, and refuse to even acknowledge Quentin and Daisy's existence.

Anyways, I wanted nothing to do with helping Quentin get Eileen back from the Ortegas. I was on the verge of telling him "no", when Danny said, "Sure. What do you got going?"

Air rushed from my lungs in a gasp, and I nearly passed out. I saw no good out of helping retrieve Eileen from the Ortegas.

"I don't expect you fellas gettin' too tangled up in this mess," said Quentin, with a cocky smile that gave me little assurance. "I just need you there, just in case some bastard pulls a blade on me."

"What if they pull a blade and Danny or me?" I asked, with a bit of sarcasm mixed with growing fear. I hated conflict, and avoided it like death. I was in no mood to get my ass handed back to me.

"Aw shit, you don't gotta worry about that!" claimed Quentin, with a dirty look. "I don't think we're gonna have much trouble with Luis or his goddamn family."

"I sure hope not," I mumbled, nervously.

"You ain't got nothin' to worry about," answered Quentin. He got up from the table, staggered to an easy chair in the corner, and fetched a beat-up, green baseball cap. "Don't take much to put beaners in their place. They talk mean and dirty, especially when they talk Spick. But when the goin' gets tough, them wetback bastards run like scared rabbits."

7

Quentin O'Roarke got in his old GMC pickup, while Danny and me followed him to the Ortegas in the van. By now, it was kind of cold and dark outside. There wasn't much rain but a sprinkle here and there. Lightning lit up the night sky far in the distance, along with loud, rumbling thunder.

Quentin's pickup was a beater, which had hauled loads of firewood and bales of hay all over the place. Quentin bought it off Uncle Ray, and still showed signs of its former owner in the empty cartons of cigarettes or smashed beer cans in the cab. The truck was a sky blue. It blew black smoke from the exhaust pipe, and had long saw better days.

The only light from inside the van was from the dashboard, or streetlights we passed on the narrow lanes to the Ortegas. As the windshield wipers slapped back and forth, a Neil Diamond song played on the radio.

"You sure this is a good idea?" I asked Danny.

"I don't think much will come of this," said Danny, calmly. "Quentin can brag and blow all he wants, but he won't lay a hand on Luis, or anyone else."

"I hope," I mumbled, anxiously.

Danny snickered. "I been with Quentin a bunch of times, when he goes off and tries to start fights. No worries, Gerry. This'll be more entertaining than anything else."

The Ortegas lived near a dead end of a gravel street, on the edge of the city limits. Their home was next to a stone wall, which separated their property from the town cemetery. The Ortegas owned a modest, one-story house with dull green shingles, and a sort-of trimmed lawn, and a cluttered garage to the left.

Luis' dad, Roberto, was around the age of fifty who, even after moving to America almost thirty years before, still couldn't speak English very good. He'd been a field hand for several landowners in both Oregon and Washington. He got hurt real bad on a job a few summers before, but never reported the injury because he was an illegal.

Luis still lived with his folks, and was their only source of income, in a house with two parents and four kids. The kids' ages ranged from nineteen to eleven. Luis was protective of his kin, and always afraid that his old man would get deported. Most people in town knew that Roberto never got his citizenship, and once in a while someone might threaten to turn him in to Immigration. Anyways, the kids were all born in America, were legal, and not prone to stir up shit.

The last thing the Ortegas needed was to have Quentin show up that night, looking to fetch Eileen back while also trying to stir up shit.

We pulled up in front of the Ortegas' house, behind Quentin.

I took a deep breath and whispered, "This won't be good. . . Trust me, Dan. This won't be good."

"Don't worry," said Danny, grinning. "The worst thing that can happen is that I might decide to put this in a story, some day...."

Danny and I stayed in the van, as Quentin got out of the pickup. He thrust his chest out like he was in charge. He took a sip from his beer, then a drag from his cigarette. He pressed on the pickup's horn, as a high-pitched wail sounded in the night.

This grabbed the attention of just about everyone around.... Including the dead who rested endlessly in their graves, behind the cemetery wall.

"Luis!" hollered Quentin, as he pressed on the horn three or four times. "Luis Fuckin' Ortega! Get yer scrawny Spick ass out here, boy! I wanna talk to you!"

Danny let out a nervous little chuckle, as fear nearly got the best of me. We weren't at the Ortegas for a pleasant little Meet and Greet.

"Luis!" hollered Quentin, once more pressing on the horn. "Get yer chickenshit Spick ass out here. And bring my fuckin' daughter with ya!"

A jolt of panic ran through my entire body, as Luis stepped outside from the front door of his house... along with Eileen O'Roarke.

Luis said nothing. He didn't have to. He stared blankly at the lunatic, raging father, standing next to a beat-up old pickup.

Eileen hopped from the porch, hotter than a scalding iron. "You son of a bitch!" she screeched, and stomped toward Quentin.

"Just who do ya think you are, calling me names?" snapped Quentin. "You knows who pays the fuckin' bills for yer lazy little twat?"

My heart skipped a beat.

"Yeah, I know," said Eileen, with her fists clenched. "Fucking Aunt Joyce, that's who! Sure as hell ain't you or Mom!"

Quentin started to say something. He got stopped by what Eileen just said. A blind man could see the shame, embarrassment, and humiliation on his face. He tried to recover from it.

Finally, after several seconds, Quentin said, "I brought you into this world, and I can by God take you out of it!"

"You couldn't hurt a fly!" laughed Eileen. "You can talk all the shit you want, but you can't even run your own fucking life!" Her voice got more and more shrill, loud, and high-pitched. "Why the fuck should I want you to run mine?"

"C'mon, get in the rig, right here and now," ordered Quentin, his tone not nearly as mean and hostile as before. "Ain't got nothin' more to say about it. Get in the rig, and we'll pretend none of this ever happened. You refuse to follow my rules, I got no choice but to call the cops, and get them involved. You want that, Eileen?"

"You want me to call the cops, and tell them of all the illegal wood you cut?" questioned Eileen. "Or all them deer and elk you poached? Or all the fish you caught out of season?" Tears dripped from Eileen's eyes. Even then, she somehow smiled. "Or your claims of being a quarter Bannock or Nez Perce, just so you can get hunting or fishing rights, not to mention a fat check from the government? You think you're hot shit! You ain't nothing but a phony, law-breaking son of a...."

Quentin slugged Eileen right on the nose, as hard as he could.

Eileen flew backwards, like she'd been hit by a high-caliber bullet. She landed butt-first into the mushy, rain-soaked lawn.

Danny and I jumped out of the van, as fast as we could. Meanwhile, Luis left his front porch, hoping to give Quentin a lesson he'd never forget.

Regrettably, Luis wasn't much better at giving lessons than Eileen was. He was a pretty good mechanic, honest, hard-working, and good to his family. But he was no fighter. He was a tall, lanky, handsome kid with hair down to his shoulders and a pencil-thin mustache, which kind of made him look dashing and debonair. But he wasn't any more skilled at bare-fisted brawling than Danny or me. The best Luis could do was call Quentin a bad name in Spanish, take a swing at his opponent's nose, and miss by a mile.

Quentin placed two of his fingers into Luis' eyes, *Three Stooges*-style.

Luis cried out, threw his hands over his face, and backed away.

A split-second later, Quentin sent one foot into Luis' balls.

Luis doubled over and fell to the ground, not far from Eileen.

"Quentin!" hollered Danny. He wrapped his arms around his cousin's torso, to keep him from stomping a mud hole into Eileen or Luis.

I got in front of Quentin, looking dumber than I normally do. Instead of being a well-meaning participant, I became a totally useless part in this scenario.

"C'mon, Quentin," urged Danny, trying to remain calm and in control. "You made your point, now let it go…"

"The hell I made my point!" hollered Quentin, reaching back to latch onto Danny's hair. "I'll make a point, a'right, with a fuckin' blade in his guts! Now get the fuck away from me!"

Danny screamed as Quentin ripped out some of his hair.

I don't know if common sense or if it was my brain which left me. Usually, my apprehension told me not to do something like this. But I just couldn't stand by and let Quentin pulverize everyone, including my soon-to-be-ex-boyfriend. My own anger and stupidity won over smarts, and before I knew what I was doing, I done it.

What did I do?

I sent my right fist into Quentin's chin, and did an absolutely fine job of proving nothing.

Quentin staggered slightly backwards, not knowing who or what had just nailed him. At first, he had to lean against the Ortegas' white-picket fence, to stay on his feet. Confusion and disbelief revealed themselves in his eyes. A few cusswords slipped from his bloody mouth. Both knees buckled. He shot a glance at me, in a way which put the fear of God in me.

At that moment, I was split between screaming like a bitch, or standing my ground in a brave, noble manner. Instead, I stood there like a half-wit and an imbecile and a moron.

Blood dripped from Quentin's lips, into his greying chin whiskers. He issued a feeble, drunken protest concerning my apparent wrongdoing.

He then picked me up like a ragdoll, lifted me over his head, and threw me across the Ortegas' yard.

Seconds later, I landed into some pink flamingoes, gnomes, and other assorted lawn ornaments.

Air swept out of my lungs, like a deflated tire. My arms, legs, and back got scraped or bruised by the various ornaments, which got flattened or shattered on impact. My knees, shoulders, and elbows got the worst of it. My vision clouded and blurred. Lightning bolts, tweety birds, and stars danced around in my fading consciousness.

I lied on the soggy grass, wheezing and gasping in order to catch a breath. My entire body hurt like hell. This is what I got, and deserved, for being such a dimwit. I was always a very slow learner, and that night proved no exception.

Quentin grabbed Luis by the hair, and lifted him from the damp, dewy ground. "Fuck gives you the right to bang a white girl? Huh? *HUH?* Answer me, ya scrawny, wetback, Mex fuck!"

I wanted to come to Luis' rescue, but couldn't. I was too busy attempting to reconnect my head to my own ass....

Roberto, Luis' old man, headed outside. He was a little guy, even smaller than me. His height never reached five feet. Sure, he wasn't a big guy, but he wasn't afraid to fight, when it came to his own kids.

My Spanish is Greek. All I know is what Roberto called Quentin probably isn't worth repeating, anyways. Anyways, Roberto had a dark complexion, black hair which greyed in places, a thick mustache and goatee, and narrow, scary eyes. He had muscles bulging on top of muscles, and a pot belly. He wore a white tee-shirt, black jeans with holes at the knees, and leather sandals.

Roberto hollered a long stream of cusswords in Spanish, which I've never heard before, and may never hear again, except in a Robert Rodriquez film.

As I lied there in the mud and the blood and the rain, I hoped Roberto was able to accomplish what others could not... beat the hell out of Quentin O'Roarke. For what it was worth, I'm glad it was Roberto to step up to the plate, and not me.

Quentin saw Roberto heading his way, in the haze and darkness of night. He smiled real big, thinking that Roberto was no match for him.

Roberto Ortega threw his entire weight into his left fist, and slammed Quentin right smack in the eye.

I heard a loud snap, crackle, and pop, as Quentin flew into the white picket fence.

Seconds later, Roberto sent a right jab into Quentin's jaw.

Quentin opened his mouth to spew a long line of cusswords. Instead, broken and decaying teeth flew out of his bloody, gaping lips.

Roberto then struck Quentin on the nose. Quentin dropped to his knees, as red and green snot exploded from his nostrils.

Roberto took a couple of steps in Quentin's direction.

He didn't expect Quentin to head-butt him in the ribs.

Roberto's eyes bulged out, as he grunted and struggled to get even.

By now, Eileen and Luis had somehow recovered from the punishment Quentin gave them earlier. Along with my soon-to-be-ex-boyfriend Danny, they ganged up on Quentin from all sides, with repeated volleys to the face, torso, arms and legs.

I would've been all-too-happy to stay there on the ground, watching this from a safe distance. Watching Quentin getting beaten and stepped on was sort of unreal, almost kind of funny, like it came out of a movie or comic book. I really wanted to get back into the van, due to all the injuries I sustained by smashing into yard gnomes and pink flamingoes. At the same time, I still thought it was wrong not to take a stand, put on a noble act, and pretend like I still gave a damn. This, as everyone else was getting their asses kicked.

I stumbled to my feet, yet found it difficult to stand. For a while, I had to lean against the garage wall to keep from collapsing. One of my knees leaked blood, from where it got hurt on a yard gnome's annoyingly smiling face. One of my front teeth felt kind of loose.

Slowly, I stepped forward to get a better look of Quentin getting trounced on by Roberto, Eileen, Luis, and my soon-to-be-ex-boyfriend Danny. I didn't get involved right at first, because it was safer that way.

Quentin flailed helplessly on the ground, screaming and squalling and howling and hollering for the others to stop beating on him. His cries for help kind of reminded me of a horrible and unforgiving day the year before, when Uncle Ray slaughtered one of the hogs. I always hated it when we had to put one of the pigs down, even for food. Even then, whenever Uncle Ray shot one of them, it was usually a clean kill, and the guest of honor never really suffered.

The one exception was when Ray pointed a *Ruger* 22 rifle at this one pig's forehead. Just then, the oinker moved just slightly and caught the bullet in the snout.

The loud, high-pitched squeals sounded like the hunger pangs of a tiny infant. The injured pig somehow managed to bust out of the pen to run all around the place, spilling blood everywhere. Ray tried to get in a good shot, and I lost track of the number of bullets the pig had in him... in his legs, his guts, a couple or three in the face, and one which grazed his ear, before he gave up the ghost and finally died. This came as I somehow managed to tackle the poor oinker, its whole body smeared in blood, as Uncle Ray slit its throat. Even then, the poor pig still lived a minute or two afterwards, until it dropped over, both eyes glazed over in death.

During this whole time, I found myself laughing hysterically, not because it was funny, but because it was so *horrible*. It was like watching the final shoot-out in *The Wild Bunch,* something you're drawn into, no matter how sickening and gruesome it all is.

Later, the hog hung from a beam in the woodshed, its steaming guts and hide given to the chickens as a feast.

I ran off to my bedroom and cried like a wimp and a whiner and a bitch for the rest of the day, and most of that night, upset by what had happened.

I never liked Quentin O'Roarke. Part of me took a certain pleasure in watching his badly-needed and well-deserved ass-kicking. He was a disgusting person, without an honest bone in his body who never had anything good to say about others.

But, as I watched everyone beat on him, his eyes met mine. Silently, he begged me to call a halt to this punishment.

Yeah, okay, so I never liked Quentin O'Roarke. It never stopped me from feeling sorry for the drunken bastard. I suddenly felt trapped, conflicted, arguing with myself on whether to join in, or coming to Quentin's rescue. Shame and guilt swept over me. Thoughts of right or wrong fought against thoughts of helplessness, hopelessness, and surrender. I couldn't see myself defending someone like Quentin.

But could I simply stand back and watch him take such a beating?

Yeah, sure, Quentin brought this on himself, and he deserved every bit of it. But when was it to call a halt to this bullshit, and decide that enough was enough?

And even if I stepped up on Quentin's behalf, how could I stop the others from taking pleasure in stomping the hell out of him?

I rolled my eyes back, took a deep breath, and somehow mustered my courage ... for entirely the wrong reasons.

"Get off of him!" I hollered.

Like an idiot, I dared to first shove Eileen, then my soon-to-be-ex-boyfriend Danny .... then Luis and finally Roberto away from Quentin, who by this time was covered with blood, footprints, loose grass and gravel, snot, piss, shit, and mud.

"Get off of *him!*" I repeated, sounding more like a weakling and not someone of authority or importance. "You're just as bad or worse than he is!"

Luis and Roberto answered this, by kicking Quentin in the ribs. Danny simply glared at me like I was stupid.

I admit that defending somebody like Quentin O'Roarke made no sense. Crying my eyes out over a dead pig probably made no sense, either. But, because I was and probably still am a moron and a weakling and a half-wit and a coward, I couldn't keep myself from constantly doing the *wrong* thing.

Luis and Roberto gave me the evil eye, then referred to me as something bad in Spanish. I still got no idea what they called me. Probably just as well. I deserved every insult and cussword hurled at me, whether I understood it or not.

I didn't expect Eileen O'Roarke to backhand me across the face.

"Gerry Fuckin' O'Fearna, you two-faced little bastard!" she screamed, looking at me like I suffered from a combination of HIV, leprosy, and questionable morality. "Sorry, sawed-off, faggot son of a bitch! How the fuck can you take his side over *mine?*"

Whoops....

"Answer me, you motherfucking gay asshole!" she cursed, loud enough for the entire city of Nez Perce to hear, through the rain and the fog and the drizzle. "How can you take his side over mine?"

I couldn't answer. I lacked the words, the wisdom, and the balls to uphold myself. All I could do was glance over at my soon-to-be-ex-boyfriend Danny, who also failed to speak.

"Who the hell sticks up for you and Danny, huh?" screeched Eileen, in pain and betrayal. "Everyone in town knows that you two love each other, no matter how fuckin' hard you try to keep it to yourselves! Half the two-faced, cunty little bitches at school laugh at you guys behind your back.... You know that? Got any clue about that, ass-fuck? Huh? *Huh?*

And who in the fuck sticks up for you, because you and my cousin are in love with each other? You fuckin' think any of these assholes will help you out, Gerry? Do *you?* Most of these assholes in this piece of shit town think you're a fuckin' joke! And here I've been trying to stick up for you, and what do you do? Take my asshole dad's side over mine .... That's *what!* So fuck you, Gerry Fuckin' O'Fearna! I never wanna fuckin' speak to you again! You got that? Why don'tcha just fuck yourself and.... and.... and fuckin' die? Fuck you, Gerry! Fuck you, fuck your whole rotten family, and fuckin' eat shit and die!"

With that, Eileen and the two Ortegas went back inside the house, and slammed the door shut behind them. This left Danny and me, standing over what was left of Quentin O'Roarke.

"Are you out of your mind?" questioned Danny. "Or *what?*"

I merely shrugged my shoulders, my thoughts still conflicted about saving Quentin's butt. I simply gave Danny a stupid look and said, "She can call me whatever she wants, but I'm pretty sure my full name's not really 'Gerry Fuckin O'Fearna'."

Danny looked over at me, then down at his battered and bruised family member. For the exception of the ear-splitting screams of a nearby train speeding through town, it was oddly quiet.

"Well, that went as well as could be expected," I commented, blankly. "Sure you wanna put all of that in your next story?"

"Why the hell not?" grunted Danny. Slowly, he lifted Quentin up, then took him to the GMC pickup.

"Fuckin' beaners," whimpered Quentin, tears dripping from his eyes. "Took my own daughter from me. My own flesh and blood! Oughta sneak over here later tonight with my fuckin' .06 and kill all these fuckin' illegal bastards..."

"C'mon, Quentin," whispered Danny, trying to comfort his drunken and ass-kicked cousin.

"Fuck you, Dan!" bawled Quentin, wiping his swollen face. "Fuck do you know about it? How can you even know what I'm even talkin' about? You'll never marry or have kids, limp-wristed fairy! Limp-wristed, fuckin' fairies! How the fuck can you understand how I'm feelin' right now?"

Danny and I traded glances. Neither of us said much. I felt real bad because I knew that Eileen and Luis were no longer on speaking terms with me. Eileen had been a very close friend, and I just blew that one big-time. I figured I had my work cut out for me, to try and mend fences with her, if I even could now. In the back of my mind, I already knew I'd spend the rest of my life regretting what I done.

"Gerry," said Danny, choosing his words carefully as he spoke. He gave me a warm smile, which could convince me of *anything*. "Do you think you can drive Quentin back over to my place, in his rig?"

"*Me?*" I gulped. "You want me to drive him back to your place.... In *his* rig?"

"I.... If you will."

"But where?... Where are you gonna be?" I asked, anxious and a bit angry and definitely worked up. I didn't like driving, I sucked at it and still do kind of suck at it. Anyways, Quentin's GMC was a stick shift, which only made things worse.

And, worse yet, I didn't have a driver's license.

Danny didn't say anything. He merely wrung his hands and shuffled his feet like some third-rate performer in a blackface and minstrel show. Finally, he answered, "Meet me at the Warriors Den. I... I'm meeting someone... some guy.... Who wants to sell me an old *Jeep*."

"An old Jeep?" I asked.

Danny nodded.

"Well, what?...." I pointed at the van. "I thought.... Well.... I thought you loved that old crate! You're not gonna sell?...."

"No," said Danny. "I'm not gonna sell the van. Don't worry, I'm keeping it. I just thought I'd head off to Portland in new wheels."

My heart sank, as again I was reminded of Danny's departure.

Danny frowned. "Well, you honestly don't expect me to hang around here for the rest of my life!"

I turned my head away, to hide the tears in my eyes.

Danny leaned over and gave me a peck on the lips. "I love you," he said, caressing my face with the palm of his hand. "See you when ya get there."

"Okay," I said, with a moronic smile. "I love you, too."

Danny hopped in his van and drove away.

Somehow, I got Quentin into the passenger side of the GMC. The whole time, he was cussing and cursing and making idle threats and feeling sorry for himself, while at the same time slobbering all over himself and me. The jerk even tried to give me a bit of a fight. Booze, along with a damned good beating, made him slightly more agreeable.

As I clipped him in with the seatbelt, Quentin sat there, whimpering and whining about Eileen "catting around with a mess o' fuckin' beaners."

"She'll be back," I said, unconvincingly. "She'll get homesick, and beg to move back in with…"

"Two-faced, fuckin' slut!"

Since my spirit animal is the American Chicken, I couldn't respond to Quentin's language with a much-needed slap to the face.

Like a lot of old pickups, Quentin's pickup was a bitch to start, and an even worse bitch to keep running. It was the nature of most of the beaters which was once owned by my Uncle Ray. Some guys just know how to fire them up, right off the bat, while the rest of us come off looking like amateurs and morons. It took me forever to get the GMC going. Quentin kept telling me to "romp" on the gas, give it plenty of juice, and time to warm up.

Once I finally got it to turn over, the GMC roared loudly and either woke up and/or pissed off the entire neighborhood. My inexperience and sheer stupidity with manual transmissions meant heading back to the O'Roarke's in first or second gear. Meanwhile, the stupid GMC died at every red light or stop sign. Then I'd have to fight to get the bitch going again, just to creep it along like a turtle or a snail.

Once we were only a mile or so from the O'Roarkes', Quentin told me to stop in a decrepit, run-down, mostly abandoned part of town.

In confusion, I did what he asked.

A little sprinkle dampened the town of Nez Perce. A foggy haze clouded and distorted my view of the world around me, which now consisted of empty stores and restaurants, victims of changing times, as most new businesses relocated to the nearby interstate or along the riverside. There were always thoughts of restoring and remodeling the older neighborhoods. Maybe it was easier for businesses and residents to buy up more choice lots, then build from scratch. No one seemed to want these out-of-date structures, with their boarded or broken windows, leaky roofs, and loose shingles blowing in the wind.

"What're we stopping here, for?" I asked, in my typical numbskull manner as I shut off the engine.

Quentin didn't say much right at first. He just sat there, staring through the rain-soaked windshield with a dreamy, yet still sad and melancholy face.

"This used to be the funnest part of town," he said finally, "before the asshole Spicks and Californians took over."

My eyes gazed upon the darkened cityscape, in a place which once was the hub of Nez Perce, with its marques, flashing lights and neon signs, which would never, could never, see their former glory. These crumbling buildings were now home to stray cats and the occasional, homeless transient. A few were scheduled for demolition.

A number of historical societies and city planners tried to buy this dying neighborhood, resurrect it, and breathe new life into it. Other folks viewed it as an eyesore, and wanted it done in, then replaced by condos, a new city park, and summer homes for summer people with their money, influence, and powerful connections.

I remember Uncle Ray and Aunt Fran and Mom talking about the different stores, diners, and taverns which lined these streets. Not far from where we parked, was a single-screen "show house". Decades before, it had been the only movie theater in town, and a great place to catch a weekend matinee, or take your sweetheart to the latest blockbuster. This was the *Columbia River Cinema,* which closed down over thirty years before. It lost out to the *Chief Joseph Theatre,* with its triplex, surround sound, and comfortable seating. It wasn't so long ago when the Chief Joseph also shut its doors, as it too got replaced by a multiplex with eight screens, 3-D options, stadium seating, and cheap afternoon showings.

The Columbia River Cinema opened during the time of Charlie Chaplin, Douglas Fairbanks, and Mary Pickford, the superstars of the silent era. Sure, this relic, with its art deco sign and huge marquee, had survived the transition from silent to talkies, black and white to color, standard screen to *Cinemascope.* But now its day was done. Soon, it would be replaced by a parking lot or a *Bi-Mart.*

In the darkness, I could barely read the remaining letters or see the shattered lights of the marquee. The last picture show to play there was a re-release of an old Walt Disney classic, *Pinocchio.*

I never went into the Columbia River Cinema. I only walked by there a few times. I had no real reason to enter these dusty streets. There was nothing to interest me. But, from what I'd been told, the show house's interior was really something, with its arched doorways, a huge lobby, and paintings or designs to put Da Vinci or Michaelangelo to shame.

The Good Ol' Days.

"Wish I could've been here when it was still hopping," I said, quietly.

"Fuck, wish you coulda too," mumbled Quentin, lighting a cigarette as he fought back tears. "But ya won't. Never have, and ya never will. This part of Nez Perce was cool when I was a kid. Me and the folks could spend a whole Saturday dinkin' around here. That is, if you could find a fuckin' parkin' spot! Hell, ever'body hung around here back then. Fuckin' ever'body! And if it wasn't with my folks, it was me and my friends! Look...." Quentin pointed somewhere off in the darkness. "Best fuckin' burgers in town was right over there! That son of a bitch diner never knew a slow fuckin' day back then! It'd go day and night, clear t' fuckin' midnight sometimes! And now look at it. Fuck, you couldn't pay a pig or a nigger to open it back up, now. Not since the asshole taco benders moved here! Sons o' bitches! Only time you'd see them sons o' bitches back then was in the summer, and most o' them had more sense than to head into town. Too busy earnin' their keep on all the farms and ranches around here, up along Walla Walla and Milton-Freewater and the Tri-Fuckin'-Cities an' shit. Fuckers knew their place back then, and kept to themselves. A man can't even head downtown now, where some damn Spick won't pull a fuckin' blade on ya. They talk shit to us born Americans like you and me in that Spick gibberish o' theirs. Fuckers won't even try to talk English! And then they shack up together, about twenty of them to a house, worse than a buncha fuckin' Dagos or Micks! Oughta line 'em all up and shoot 'em!"

I let out a sigh, knowing where this was going. Blame the Mexicans for everything! All I wanted to do now was get Quentin home, head to the Warriors Den, and spend the rest of the night with my soon-to-be-ex-boyfriend Danny. What I wouldn't do to spend another five minutes or so in the back of his van, on that dirty, dusty, musty old mattress, where so many memories were made between us! I bothered me knowing that Danny was leaving for Portland in just a few days, and I wondered when or if we'd get a chance to do the nasty again.

Little did I know that Quentin had a loaded, *Smith and Wesson* .357

sitting in the seat next to him, buried under a pile of gun and girly maga-zines.

Without so much as a warning, Quentin opened his big mouth, shoved the muzzle of that hand cannon between his teeth, and cocked the hammer back.

Right at first, I didn't know what the hell was going on. Quentin just sat there, shaking like a leaf. One finger slowly crept to the trigger.

My eyes widened from alarm and fear. I knew I had to do some-thing.... But what?

The next few seconds.... If I even had the luxury of the next few sec-onds.... Were strange and unspeakable. Images of brains and bone spray-ing on me nearly drove me to get clear of the GMC's cab. My heart skipped a beat, as I released a frightened gasp.

Quentin's hands tightened around the pistol grip, as one finger sneaked, closer and closer, to the trigger.

"No!" I shrieked loudly. I reached out at Quentin's boney grasp, won-dering how I'd remove the pistol from his gaping mouth.

The explosive sounds of a gunshot sounded in the tiny confines of the enclosed cab. The sudden flash of muzzle fire illuminated the darkness of night. It was as if Satan cackled mercilessly at the world around me.

I let out a shriek, as the *BOOM* nearly shattered my eardrums... to be replaced by a deafening silence and severe ringing.

Panic was in charge now.

A section of the cab's roof shattered above me. Upholstery and steel scattered everywhere. Shards of hot metal struck my face, hands, and bare legs. I covered both of my ears, and spilled out a string of cusswords which ran together on a wild, chaotic, and incoherent manner.

It was the second time that night I saved Quentin O'Roarke's useless, pitiful life... at the expense of my hearing and rattled nerves.

Quentin sat next to me, piss running down the pant legs of his torn, faded sweats. I laughed hysterically, not because it was funny, but just *because.*

This soon gave way to anger and fury.

"What the fuck?" Quentin whispered to himself. He let go of a Bronx cheer which stunk up everything, like he just got done shitting himself. "What the *fuck?!?* Am I still alive?"

"You fucking are, ass wipe!" I hollered, my heart racing out of control. "But you fucking shouldn't be!"

I ripped the pistol from Quentin's quivering hands, opened the door, and hopped outside. "Try that again, asshole," I added, in a maniacal voice, "and I'll fucking kill you!"

After slamming the pickup door, I soon found myself sprinting down the abandoned street, the smoking gun in my hand. I had no idea where I was going, or what I'd do once I got there. I was just some dumb, frightened kid, running down the street with a .357, like I had just left the scene of a crime.

"O'Fearna!" Quentin roared out, from behind me. "Get back here, you miserable ... Gimme my fuckin' gun, you cheap, buttfuckin' little cunt!"

In the distance, sirens screamed loudly, as a couple of cop cars sped in my direction. Desperately, I searched for some place.... *Any place....* To hide the pistol. Let Quentin explain the massive hole in the GMC's roof. The last thing I wanted was to get caught with the .357, which Quentin tried to kill himself with.

Looking all around, I quickly placed the gun in a nearby mailbox, then darted to the closest alleyway I could find. In the misty fog and slight drizzle, I made a hasty run to the Warriors Den, where my soon-to-be-ex-boyfriend Danny waited for me.

8

It was sprinkling as I headed to the Warriors Den. By now, nightfall had completely overtaken the city of Nez Perce. Traffic was sort of heavy, even with the crummy weather. The streetlights held an eerie effect on the town, as the fog and drizzle gave everything a surreal look and feel. There was a definite smell of fall in the air. Already, trees were losing their leaves, and colored in hues of orange, brown, yellow and red. In the dampness, I felt a chill coming on. A cool breeze swept in from the river. It crept into the legs of my shorts, where my thighs and crotch caught the blunt of it. Moisture worked through my hooded sweatshirt and tee-shirt. I now regretted this trip into town, even if I got to spend time with my soon-to-be-ex-boyfriend Danny.

I don't know why I did and still like to wear shorts, even in the lousy weather. I'd sometimes put on a pair of *Carhartt* overalls that my Uncle Ray gave me, and wander to school in them. Once I got to my destination, I'd take off the overalls then spend the day in shorts.

Mom always fretted about me "freezing my poor little legs off," while Aunt Fran regarded me as "some kind of a nut." Then Uncle Ray would say that I wore shorts so I could "run away from some cute Mexican wom-

     Doug McKim

an or negro girl."

I admit that, during that cold rainy night in Nez Perce, a pair of long pants would've been nice. My shoes and socks got real soggy from all the mud puddles I ran through, while I got away from Quentin O'Roarke.

Anyways, for some reason the closer I got to the Warriors Den, the more nervous I got. I don't know why, but something in the back of my mind told me I wouldn't like what I saw, when I got there.

I didn't like it then, and I still don't like it now.

Just as I got to the Warriors Den parking lot, I spotted Danny in the front seat of his van. And he wasn't alone.

At first I smiled when I saw my ex-boyfriend, a smile which left me when I saw him kissing someone next to him.

I couldn't believe my eyes. I simply couldn't believe me fucking eyes! I thought they were playing tricks on me... or maybe I just hoped they were. I couldn't believe Danny.... My beloved Danny... was cheating on me. But he was!

I stared, silent and still, through a rain-covered windshield, as Danny's lips met another guy's lips.

I couldn't believe it! I simply couldn't fucking believe it! My heart sank. At the same time it beat, wildly, out of control, inside me. My hands got clammy and sweaty, my lips were dry, and both eyes were teary from sadness and shock. I refused to believe what I just saw.

I nearly dropped over dead, and had to lean against a bike rack to keep from falling over. It seemed like my whole life had drained out of me. I lacked the strength, the will, the desire, and the courage to move on.

My idiotic heart made me love Danny O'Roarke. Hopes and dreams couldn't accept thoughts that he'd ever desert me. It wasn't just the knowing that that Danny was soon heading off to a new life in Portland. He was deserting me... or maybe he already deserted me, for the lips, arms, and warmth of another.

Suddenly, I wanted to kill Danny O'Roarke.... Or did I want to kill myself?

Tears spilled from my eyes, and mixed with the rain which covered my cheeks. I buried my face under the palms of both hands. I started to cry, which led to a shrill, high-pitched shriek.

I wanted to run from the Warriors Den, but my legs just wouldn't carry me.

I then found myself kneeling upon the wet, muddy ground, bawling like a baby. Danny O'Roarke was leaving me! Clearly, he already had. This, despite what we had done earlier. The ecstasy we shared while making love and holding tight to each other, gave way to the most painful of truths. My love for Danny O'Roarke meant everything to me. Yet, his love for me didn't mean a damned thing to him, other than a cheap little thrill, while he thrusted himself, over and over and over again, into me.

Son of a bitch!

Goddamn, motherfucking son of a bitch!

Thoughts of fetching Uncle Ray's 30.06 from his gun cabinet, then emptying it into Danny while saving one last bullet for myself overwhelmed me. I wanted to end my life, and Danny's, praying that that the bastard found some level of humility, shame, and guilt in the afterlife. As for me, I didn't care if I gained resurrection in Heaven, or a fiery pit in Hell. I didn't care if I fucking slept for all eternity, assuming I'd be set free from the pain seething through every inch of my soul, spirit, and body. Nothing else mattered at that point. I only wanted out, forever.

"Gerry?" a girl's voice called for me, in the fog, rain, and darkness. "Gerry? Are you all right?"

I looked up to see Morgan Petrie standing over me. Her image was clouded by the tears in my eyes.

Morgan knelt beside me, and placed one hand on my shoulders. "Gerry!" she hollered. "What's wrong?"

I opened my mouth to speak. Only a helpless whimper slipped out.

"Let's go inside," said Morgan, motioning to the restaurant's door. "C'mon. Let's go inside, where it's warm and you can tell me all about it."

I shook my head and mouthed 'no.'

Morgan took my hand and practically dragged me to the entrance.

Right about then, Danny jumped from the van. He looked like he just got done screwing the cat (or somebody else). "Gerry... Gerry wait!" he spoke. "We gotta talk!"

I glanced over at the van to see my ex-boyfriend's new boyfriend. I didn't know the bastard, nor did I want to know him. It was enough to know that Danny was no longer a part of my life. He found himself another, someone I was totally ignorant of.

Well, he wasn't a bad-looking fella, I'm guessing right around nineteen or twenty, with long, black hair, a dark complexion, and deep-set eyes. He wore a blue, plaid shirt, and jeans. From a distance, he kind of looked like a Native-American, and I wondered if he once lived on the Umatilla Reservation near Pendleton. The guy never said a word to me, and seemed kind of confused and perplexed. Chances were he never even knew I existed. Maybe Danny played the field against him, too. What might of ran through his mind at that given moment, I'll never know.

Part of me wanted to run straight back into Danny's arms, praying to win him back by showering him with kisses. Part of me wanted to send the miserable bastard flying into the middle of next week. All of me wanted to understand what was going on, and ask *why?.... Why? .....*

Why was Danny with another guy?

I sought love, appreciation, and approval by holding tight to Morgan Petrie. This, as an ocean of tears flowed down my cheeks.

"Gerry!" Danny cried out. "Gerry, please wait.... We gotta talk...."

The sound of Danny calling my name only made things worse. I tightened my grip around Morgan, as my pleas grew louder and more emotional.

"C'mon, Gerry," Morgan told me. "I'll fix you a hot chocolate...."

I went into the Warriors Den, where it was nice, warm, and dry.... Yet still lonely and heartbreaking. Morgan led me to a booth, by a large window facing the nearby highway.

Moments later, Danny wandered inside. He stood by the door, staring at me. I stared back, until the misery of it all got the better of me, and I found myself blubbering like a baby in my hot chocolate. This, as others gawked at me in wonderment, concern, or vile, mean-spirited humor.

Danny slowly approached me, knowing he done wrong. Whether he was willing to admit it or not, that was another thing. For me, this ranked as one of the worst days of my life. Although everyone and their dog in the Warriors Den knew I was and still am gay, I didn't want that to be the night's entertainment.

A few schoolmates laughed at me. Had there been any question whether Danny and me were an item, that pretty much answered it. It didn't help when someone mumbled, "Lovers' quarrel," while others responded in chuckles.

Danny pretended to ignore it. Still, it bothered him. As Danny got closer and closer, sadness almost devastated him, too.

The harder I struggled to hide the pain, the worse it got. The closer Danny got, the more I carried on like the whiny little bitch that I was.

"Can I?.... Can I sit down?" Danny whispered.

I didn't answer, in fears of blowing up and making things worse.

Danny looked over at Morgan, who simply glared at him. I think she wanted to rip his head off. Morgan had been a good friend for an awful long time. She hated seeing me get hurt, and wanted to get back at the one responsible.... In this case, Danny O'Roarke.

"I.... I meant to tell you earlier," said Danny, daring to take a seat on the other side of the table. "I met someone up in Portland...."

Defeated by his own conflicted mind, Danny turned a beet-red, as he hunted for the words that didn't come.

Well, what difference did it make, now? Danny met someone up in Portland. I was out on my ass, and making a fool of myself in the Warrior's Den.

Danny reached out to take my hand, but I pulled back.

Danny wiped away a tear or two. "Gerry…. I meant to tell you earlier, but…"

"Did you also mean to fuck my brains out in your ugly-ass van, before telling me?" I hollered, unable to keep my voice down. "Get your god-damn thrills out on me, before we broke up?"

Danny said nothing. He looked away, too ashamed to say much.

"I suppose what we did together doesn't mean a thing to you, does it?" I hollered. "I thought you loved me, and proved it by banging me…"

"Gerry!" Danny cut in, frantically. *"Shhh!"*

"What makes you think I give a shit, now?" I cried, getting louder and louder and not caring who heard. "You never gave a shit about me, did you? All you cared about was getting an easy poke out of me!" Tears fell like rain. I was upset, and wanted Danny to know exactly how I felt. "I loved you!" I screamed, both hands shaking uncontrollably as my lips quivered. "First you fuck me, then you fuck me over. Is that it?"

"Do we have to talk about it, here?" questioned Danny, nervously.

"I loved you! I thought you knew that! Is that how you treat all of your fucking boyfriends? How many times have you cheated on 'Mr. Broke-back Mountain', waiting out in your goddamn van? Want me to go out and tell him what we did, just a few hours ago? Lemme guess. You two were going at it while you made me babysit your crazy asshole cousin, right? You wanted me to drive Quentin home, so you could ram your cock into your new boyfriend, from motherfucking Portland?"

"Jessey already knows," sighed Danny, staring blankly at the tile floor. "I already told him about you and me.... And about us." Danny's throat tightened. "I knew this was our last night together, and I.... I wanted it to be really special for you, for the both of us... before I left town."

"Son of a bitch," I cussed, shaking my head in disgust.

"I gotta get on with my life, and my life as a writer!" hollered Danny. "If you had the balls, you'd do something with your art!"

"Go fuck yourself!"

"Go fuck myself?" responded Danny, with a half-way, crooked grin. "Is that the best you can come up with? Go fuck myself? You're a damned good artist, Gerry, and I want you to do something cool with it! I want you to get out of this shitty little town, get real about the arts, and make something of yourself! As it is, I don't think you'll ever move out of your aunt and uncle's place, let alone Nez Perce...."

"That's my business," I mumbled, weakly, "isn't it?"

"Just like I guess it's my business if I just go ahead and come out with it," said Danny. "Goodbye, Gerry. I loved you as a companion, and I still love you as a friend." Unable to hold back, Danny also got weepy. "But I just gotta get on with my life...."

"Without me?"

"I met Jessey when I signed up for classes, a month ago," said Danny. "I dunno, I guess we both love writing, and literature, and we both want to get published, and.... Well... The next thing I knew..."

"Spare me the fucking details," I said, between clenched teeth. I was sick of myself, of Danny O'Roarke, of life in Nez Perce, and sick of life as a whole. I thought strongly of leaving the Warriors Den, right there and then, then either throw myself into the river, or walk the center line of 395 until a Wal-Mart truck or something got me out of my misery, with a sudden and quick *SMACK!* I was nothing but a miserable, sad, shy gay kid from nowhere, with no life, no prospects, no hope, nothing. Not a fucking thing. So what if I died that exact same evening? Danny just pounded the final nail into my coffin. So what? There was nothing left to do now, but arrange my own demise.

But, before I went along my merry fucking way, I wanted to give Danny something very *SPECIAL*....

"Well, since we're parting company," I said, "I want to give you a going-away present."

With that, I threw my cup of hot chocolate in Danny O'Roarke's face.

The next thing I knew, Danny sent the back of his hand into *my* face.

The next thing I knew, *my* face struck the dusty, dirty floor of the Warriors Den.

Danny stormed from the restaurant, hot chocolate dripping from *his* face, as onlookers laughed their asses off and made rude comments at the both of us.

Danny turned around to see me squirming around like a worm on the floor. "Hope you have a rotten life!" he hollered. "Rotting away in this rotten little town!"

With that, Danny O'Roarke stepped out of the Warriors Den, back to the van with Mr. Brokeback Mountain, and out of my narrow existence, and out of my life.

Morgan and a twerpy-looking kid named Derek Macready ran over to where I laid on the floor.

I was devastated that Danny and me were no longer an item, along with the knowledge that my actions with the hot chocolate were not the last word.

"What happened?" cried Derek. He was a Freshman at the high school. He had curly red hair, round, steel-framed glasses, a freckled face, and a pugged nose. He was kind of a nerd and a freak and a geek, but still kind of a pretty good guy.

I heard that Derek was like Danny and me, meaning he was of a "questionable persuasion" when it came to the nasty. I never asked him, he never told me. He wasn't exactly my type, anyways.

"Danny promised me he'd never leave me," I whimpered, my face as well as my thoughts stinging. "He *promised* me he'd never leave me!"

"So, what happened?" asked Morgan, helping me to my wobbly feet.

"He left me!" I bawled, refusing to conceal the pain from my watery eyes and high-pitched voice.

"There's other fish in the sea," said Morgan, as she returned me to the booth. "I won't tell my manager what you just did with that cup of hot chocolate. Just don't make it a habit."

"I won't," I mumbled, my words barely heard under the loud conversation and sounds of *Andrew Jackson Jihad* on the jukebox. "Sorry, Morgan."

"Don't apologize," said Morgan, with a laugh. "Danny had it coming and, besides, you're paying for the next one."

I somehow snickered at my own expense.

"You can do better than Danny O'Roarke," said Morgan.

"I doubt it," I said, on the verge of blubbering like a baby.

"Trust me, you can do better than Danny. If you don't believe me, I'll introduce you to my cousin Eliot from La Grande. I'll try to get him up here, so you two can meet."

I shrugged my shoulders. Eliot or no Eliot, I was too busy missing Danny, and feeling sorry for myself. Thoughts of jumping off the bridge which connected Oregon with Washington dominated my chaotic mind. Or maybe I'd throw myself in front of a fast-moving semi, or maybe I'd hang myself from one of the rafters in the barn, or maybe I'd use one of Uncle Ray's pistols to blow my own fucking head off.

While the pistol would be faster and hopefully less painful, I'd spray bones and brains all over the bedroom, and destroy my cherished Frazetta prints.

Of course, that gruesome sight just might put my own lame-ass attempts of art to shit and shame.

Anyways, I saw no point in carrying on with my own pitiful, useless existence.

I remembered the exact moment when I came to realize that I was and still am gay. I responded with sobs, tears, and pleas to an unknown, unseen, invisible god. I prayed never to be *like that*. Images of seeing myself swinging from a rope, above where the chickens went to roost, ruled over me. Had it not been for my relationship to Danny, I might have ended it all, months before.

Well, Danny was no longer a part of my life, so I no longer wanted to be a part of this world. All I saw now was eternal darkness. Hopes of living a happy life seemed remote, faded, distant, and out of reach. What others might have been saying about Danny and me meant nothing now. Let the bastards have fun with their asshole jokes and rumors!

Dreams of making a name and a reputation as an artist no longer mattered. Friends and family in Nez Perce seemed nil. I saw myself as a dead man walking, as the Grim Reaper eagerly awaited his victory over me. I even saw myself reading my own obituary in the *Nez Perce Republican Herald*.... If the local paper even bothered reporting on my demise!

But what the hell? I deserved to die, once Danny said his goodbye to me, the same way I deserved my perilous journey from the booth to the floor, at the Warriors Den.

With the rain, the fog, the darkness of night, I decided it was time to start my long walk back to Ray and Fran's, while praying I'd die along the way.

I got up from my seat and headed for the door.

"Where are you going?" asked Morgan. "I planned on giving you a ride home, once I got done cleaning up."

"Don't bother," I said, bluntly.

"What?" Morgan grinned, even when my stinko attitude upset her. "I don't want you walking in this awful weather. Wait here. We'll be closed in an hour, and I'll take you home when we're done with...."

"I can make it!" I hollered. I hated being rude to someone who'd been so nice to me. Still, I had a meeting with *THE END,* so why keep that appointment waiting?

"Be my guest.... I guess...." Morgan frowned. "They're calling on more rain for tonight, Gerry, and you'll get drenched."

"It won't be the first time," I said, ruder than I intended.

I stepped outside, into the cold, damp breeze.

The first thing I noticed was that Danny's van was gone. But did that really matter? Danny was no longer on speaking terms with me. Any hopes of reconciliation were long gone. I imagined that Danny was off somewhere, pumping on Mr. Brokeback Mountain, the same way he pumped on me just a short while before. Just the thought of it tore at my very soul. It made me that much more willing to become fish bait in the Columbia River.

The rain got steadily worse as I wandered through town, to the highway heading toward Ray and Fran's place.

As the weather got worse and worse, so did my pain and heartache. My mood got more and more downbeat, to the point where I honestly didn't care if I lived or died. With each passing step came the urge to scream my anger and sadness, for the whole world to hear (or at least the citizens of Nez Perce, Oregon!).

By the time I got a few blocks from the Warriors Den, I let out a bunch of high-pitched shrieks, sure to frighten or annoy everyone around me. Once I got to the road heading to my aunt and uncle's, my throat was sore and hoarse, my eyes wild from sheer madness, my clothes soaked from the rain.

Instead of going east toward home, I considered going north to the bridge. There, I'd make a hole in the mighty Columbia, and forever end this horrible, pathetic excuse of a life.

At least once a year, some sad, sorry person would throw themselves from the bridge, to be found with an acute and irreversible case of *DEAD*. Sometimes, they'd get ground up by one of the hydro-electric dams downstream. Oh, well. Dead was dead, and soon Gerry O'Fearna would be one of many sad, sorry persons who met their doom in the deep abyss of the river.

Gusts of wind chilled me. By now, I probably freaked out or pissed off quite a number of folks, who suffered the misfortune of hearing my loud shrieks. I had gone completely off my rocker, and the only thing to do now was take the plunge.

I lacked the courage or stupidity of carrying out my self-destruction. I was freezing my ass off, and wished I'd taken Morgan up on her offer to drive me home. There, I'd take a bottle of sleeping pills, or hang myself with a towel in the shower... after giving myself one last hand job, in the warm embrace of Righty and Lefty.

Heading east, I saw the bright lights of the McNary Dam, spanning across the river. The power plant's endless hums competed with the sounds of the pouring rain on black pavement. Staring at the massive structure of concrete and steel, I was reminded that my dad died on the job there, which made me feel even more crummy. Maybe I'd meet him in the Great Beyond.... Or maybe not.

Pondering the reality of my inevitable passing, I wondered if I'd go to Heaven, or in Hell, or if Death was just an endless *nothing*. Fear swept over me, to be won over by a desire to say "fuck it" and simply die.

I then felt a buzzing in the left pocket of my shorts, followed by the ringing of a cell phone. This knocked me out of my self-imposed self-pity, self-loathing, and self-hating shittery.

I retrieved the phone from my pocket, and placed it to my ear. "Hello?" I said, wondering who'd be calling me at that time.

"Gerry?" my mom cried, frantic and panicked as she practically screamed at me. *"Gerry?"*

"Yes, Mom," I said, thinking that yet another resident at the nursing home had kicked the bucket, and I was destined and doomed to hear about it. "What?.... What's up?"

"It.... It's...." stuttered Mom, her words broken by uncontrolled sobbing and boo-hooing. "It's...."

"What is it?" I asked, somehow forgetting about my own problems. "What's wrong?"

This was followed by silence, which was then followed by more whining, whimpering, and bawling... which was then followed by a hysterical shriek which nearly shattered my eardrums.

"Mom...." I said, no longer fretting about Danny, or my heartbreak, or the McNary Dam, or the cold, or the Columbia River, or my future plans of swallowing pills or shooting myself in front of the rabbits and chickens. "Mom.... What's *wrong?"*

"I just got a call from Aunt Fran," said Mom. "Ray's had another heart attack!"

"Oh, hell," I gasped, looking skyward into the hazy darkness, as raindrops hit my face. The earth was seemingly pulled out from under my feet. My entire body found itself in an unknown, uncertain, and unpredictable freefall. "How bad?... How bad is he?"

"Fran's with him at Good Shepherd," said Mom, on the verge of losing it. "And he's not good..."

9

A lot of time has passed now, since that rainy night I broke up with my now-ex-boyfriend Danny O'Roarke. And so much has happened since then.

It seems like my former life had ended that day in September, just to be replaced by a new life, a new existence, and a new beginning.

After Mom called me, I headed back to the Warriors Den, my thoughts filled with worry. Morgan treated me to another hot chocolate, which didn't end up in Danny's face. Meanwhile, I paced up and down the restaurant floor, until Mom showed up to get me.

Uncle Ray died just a few minutes past three that next morning, with Mom and Aunt Fran and a couple of close friends by his side. I refused to go into his room, to see his final moments. I just plain couldn't be there. Guess I was too much of a coward and a wussy and a pussy and a chicken to see someone die. Anyways, I just didn't need to see that.

What the hell difference did it make? Ray never woke back up. From what I heard, everything was normal. The next thing Fran knew, Ray suddenly collapsed from his easy chair to the floor. He'd been watching *Duel at Diablo* with a bottle of Henry Weinhard's in one hand and a Lucky

Strike in the other.

While I felt real bad about not going in there to see Uncle Ray kick the bucket, I still felt kind of okay for missing it. I spared myself a head full of bad memories.

Right at first, I never cried. I just couldn't. I was too far in shock to accept or admit that the old bastard was really gone.

Once me, Mom, and Aunt Fran got home, I went about doing my chores, without anyone telling me what to do or how to do it, or asking if I was worth a shit while doing it.

Aunt Fran pretended to get tough about Uncle Ray dying. She got on the phone and called just about everybody she knew, and went through a little black book of phone numbers and addresses she kept handy.

She insisted and still insists on using a land-line, where she gossips with all of her lady friends on an old rotary telephone, with its winding cord leading to the receiver. Neither her nor Ray threw anything away, if they thought it still had some use in it. Guess that's why Ray held onto that ugly old pickup, which still sits lifeless in the barn to this very day.

Aunt Fran tried to act all brave and strong, while she told everyone that Uncle Ray was gone. She pasted a phony-ass grin on her face, while she done the telling. She fixed meals like she always did, while harping at me for wearing shorts and freezing my poor little legs off in the cold. She also cussed Uncle Ray out for not being there, when she really needed his "loud mouth and lazy ass".

No surprise that Mom went through the first month or so in an endless boo-hoo. She asked for time-off from work, and never went back. She never did return to that nursing home in Hermiston. A co-worker of hers practically gave us an old *Fleetwood* mobile home, sitting in a trailer park and apartment complex in La Grande known as *Shady Nook*. It sat within spitting distance from the railroad tracks, and shook real bad whenever a train went by.

Anyways, Mom and me finally got on our feet, packed up most of our stuff, and headed off to a new town and a new life.

It took us forever to pack our stuff and move. We ended up yard-saleing a lot of it, or donating it to the *Salvation Army* or *Goodwill*. Some of it just got left behind.

We left Nez Perce, Oregon, though we still headed back now and then to see if Aunt Fran was okay, without Uncle Ray and his Lucky Strikes.

A missed a lot of people in Nez Perce. I even kind of missed Uncle Ray, even if I didn't get all teary-assed and boo-hoo about his dying. Not right at first. I just couldn't get through the idea of his being gone. I could still sometimes hear his booming voice and his snide comments about me getting mixed up with "some pretty little Mexican woman or fat negro girl" who wanted to get me down and mess with me.

It wasn't until I went digging through my wallet, and found the twenty bucks he gave me that morning right before he died. I don't know why, but finding that money did a number on me. I wasn't worth a shit to anybody or even myself, for the rest of the day.

I ran upstairs to my old bedroom in Nez Perce, where I bawled and boo-hooed and carried on like a whiny little bitch, until sometime that next day.

Then I headed to the Warriors Den and spent that twenty bucks on a couple of burgers and greasy fries, and ate like a real oinker.

Most of Uncle Ray's stuff was sold or got divvied up in the will, mainly to family and friends in the area. Aunt Fran gave up on most of the critters on the place, except for a few chickens. She made a few extra bucks selling the eggs, and had her hens to keep her company on long, lonely days, when she missed Uncle Ray the most.

10

I spent my last few months of high school in La Grande, where I sort-of, kind-of, maybe made a few chums but mostly stayed to myself. My sanctuary was in a cramped little space, at the end of a narrow hallway in the trailer, alone with my artwork and my movie posters and my love and admiration of Frank Frazetta and Norman Rockwell.

I hated being "the new kid" at La Grande High. Very few people really tried to make friends with me, which was mainly okay by me. It gave me more time to work on my pastels that I shared with those who I figured wouldn't make fun of me over them.

My end of the trailer shook like an earthquake, any time a train went by. The roof leaked real bad in the rain and snow, even after we paid to have new tar or fiberglass applied to it.

Anyways, the trailer was warm, cozy.... And it was ours.

Mom soon got a job at a nearby assisted living facility, where she still got all teary-assed and boo-hooed whenever an old person died over there. She made all right money, enough to pay the rent and buy food at the local dollar store.

One day in late-November of my senior year, I was walking home from school when I met up with another kid, just outside of the parking lot. "Pardon me," he said, with a real nice smile. "Are you Gerald O'Fearna?"

"Yeah," I said, a bit confused. "I'm Gerry O'Fearna."

I looked the kid up one side and down the other. I wondered if I saw him someplace before, maybe in the hallway or the cafeteria. Sure, I'd seen the kid around a time or two, but never gave him much thought. He was kind of short, but not near as short as me, but not near as tall as Danny. He had dark, curly hair, a fair complexion, a great smile, and beautiful green eyes, which were totally impossible to ignore. He wasn't exactly skinny, but far from being fat. He was someone Uncle Ray would describe as being a little brick shithouse, more muscle than anything else. He carried himself with ease and confidence, and I couldn't help but to admire and envy him.

He wasn't exactly the best-looking kid in the world, but he wasn't ugly neither. His face was a bit too round, his nose a bit too pugged, but still a fairly handsome guy. Somehow, he sent off a certain charm and charisma, which got my attention and kept it.

"Yeah, I'm Gerry O'Fearna," I repeated, a bit nervously. "Uhmmm... Who're you?"

"Eliot Munro," the kid said, shaking my hand. "I'm Morgan's cousin.... Y' know.... Morgan Petrie, from Nez Perce...."

"Oh, yeah!" I hollered, excitedly. "Morgan told me all about you, right before I moved down here!"

"All about me?" asked Eliot, with a grin. "I hope she wasn't *that* honest!"

"Don't worry. She said mostly nice things. *Mostly.*"

Eliot snickered. *"Mostly."*

"So.... Are you busy?" I asked, wanting to get to know Eliot better.

"Not really," said Eliot. "Got time for a burger and a Coke?"

"I got nothing but time!" I said, eager to spend part of the day with Eliot. It seemed that life in La Grande was lonely and depressing, where even the countless TV channels couldn't entertain you. "So... where's the best place in town?"

"The Golden Tiger," suggested Eliot.

"The Golden Tiger?" I asked. "Isn't that like an Oriental restaurant?"

"Sure."

"A burger and a Coke? In an Oriental restaurant?"

"You ever try a hamburger in an Oriental restaurant?" snickered Eliot.

"Uh.... No," I said.

"Then don't knock it!" laughed Eliot, slapping me on the back.

With nothing else to lose but my dinner, I tucked my textbooks under one arm and tagged along with Eliot Munro.

The wind was cold and blustery in La Grande, as usual. There was a gray haze in the skies above. It held the chilly air in the Grande Ronde Valley, which was mostly surrounded by high mountains and dense woodlands of the *Wallowa Whitman National Forest.*

I fell back into my old habit of wearing sweatshirts and shorts, and my legs caught the blunt of the nasty weather. As always, Mom whined and whimpered and carried on about my "poor little legs." Anyways, I didn't have to catch hell from Aunt Fran anymore, which was okay by me. Anyways, my face and legs got awful cold, before Eliot and me got to the restaurant on Adams Avenue, along the main drag in La Grande.

Eliot and me went into the dimly-lit joint, with a narrow walkway lined on both sides by booths. The place wasn't really busy at the time. A cute little Chinese waitress led us to a secluded table in the back, where hopefully we could talk privately. Up until then, Eliot and me never really said much, mainly just small talk about my life up in Nez Perce, before I moved down to La Grande. Anyways, the whole time I found myself drawn to him in some way, and wondered if something might come of it.

The restaurant was nice, warm, and cozy. An old *Eagles* song played from a stereo, while a few people gawked at a huge widescreen TV over the counter. The Portland Trailblazers played against some other team, which I couldn't recognize since I don't follow basketball or any other sport which I never cared about anyways. Anyways, the cute little waitress took Eliot and me to a nice little booth in the back, where we could sort-of, kind-of, maybe talk in private.

While I sort-of, kind-of, maybe got acquainted with Eliot during our short, windy stroll to the restaurant, I really wanted to get to know him better. I wasn't sure exactly sure how to break the ice, and my anxiety and lousy self-esteem almost got the better of me.

"Morgan told me you're really into painting and pastels," said Eliot, smiling real big as he took a seat across the table from me.

I didn't expect that sort of question from Eliot so soon. His willingness to get to the point almost made me jump. At first, I didn't know how to answer, so I really didn't answer at all.

"I'd love to see what you got going," said Eliot, his eyes begging with me to give him a chance to look at my artwork, and figure if it was worth a shit. "Can I?"

My heart skipped a beat, and I felt a huge lump in my throat. My fingers tingled, and all of a sudden I had an urge to run, screaming, from the restaurant. Instead, I got a stupid look on my face, as I tried but failed to say something smart, stupid, weird, or retarded. I tried to talk, but the words just didn't come.

"I won't say anything bad about it," said Eliot. Softly, he patted my hand, which felt warm and assuring. "I promise."

Somehow, I got up enough courage to look Eliot straight in the eye. I wanted to believe that he'd like my artwork. Still, I was too nervous and scared to show him much. The idiot grin on my face changed to an even dumber one, which then changed to a frown.

"Oh, c'mon!" laughed Eliot. "It can't be that bad! Can it?"

Thinking I had nothing more to lose but my pride and dignity, I scrounged through my duffle bag until I came to a pastel of a dragon... the same dragon I worked on before my last date with my now ex-boyfriend Danny, and the same dragon I worked on before Uncle Ray died. It was still in my sketchbook, and was not quite yet finished. I never got back to it since that rainy, cold day in September.

Nervously, I handed the sketchbook over to Eliot, my sweaty hands shaking like leaves. My eyes resembled that of a deer's caught in the headlights. I was afraid of baring my soul by showing my lousy artwork which I thought was "never worth a shit." I was sure that Eliot would badmouth my dragon, laugh at my childish dreams of being an artist, and forever devastate me, while killing any chances of me being a success. I just knew that he'd have nothing good to say about the dragon, and I'd remain a nothing, a nobody, and lost in a sea of obscurity by my own making.

Eliot's eyes looked the dragon over, four ways from Sunday. He never said much right at first, which made me just know that he was about to tear it all to pieces, laugh in my face, and remind me that I wasn't worth a shit, and never would be. Deliberately, I looked at the cute little waitress, who greeted more patrons to the restaurant and led them to a table. My hopes begged that Eliot would love the pastel. My fears told me that he'd hate it, worse than the crummy weather outside.

"It's awesome, Gerry!" Eliot shouted out, loud enough for everyone in the restaurant to hear. "Ever think about making a living doing this kinda stuff?"

I gasped. I'd been told by several people in Nez Perce that I was a good artist.... Mainly my ex-boyfriend Danny O'Roarke. Very few people in La Grande knew of my dreams of making a living in the arts, for the exception of Mom and a few nosey neighbors in Shady Nook. Maybe a lot of people knew I was a pretty good artist, or even *believed* I was. The problem was, I didn't believe it, nor did I want to believe it.

Danny always bugged me about not getting my stuff "out there." It upset me knowing that maybe the bastard was right, at least about that. I was my own worst enemy, and needed to get over it, if I was to ever be worth a shit as an artist or anything else.

Eliot leafed through the other pastels in my sketchbook, which mostly involved muscle-bound brutes of the "Frank Frazetta-variety", scantily-dressed damsels-in-distress, knights in blood-soaked armor, and mythological creatures like dragons (yeah, more *dragons!)*, unicorns, wizards, and fairies.

Eliot's eyes perked up every time he gazed upon yet another pastel, and his grin got bigger and bigger with each new discovery hidden in my sketchbook. Each time he turned the page, he'd gawk at another example of my work. His voice got louder and louder, and more high-pitched, until the cute little waitress had to tell him to keep his voice down. Even then, his comments raised my spirits, to the point where I actually shed a few tears in happiness.

On top of that, I now hoped, and believed, that my new friendship with Eliot Munro might grow into something more magical, more meaningful, and more special than I dared to imagine.

"So...." mulled Eliot, in admiration. "Do you got anything more I can look at?"

"Yeah," I said, without a second thought. "At my house!"

Eliot grinned in admiration. "That's not too far from here," he said, "is it?"

"Only a short walk from here," I said. "I can get there in about fifteen minutes."

"Great." Eliot's smile got bigger and bigger. "Mind if I tag along with you?"

I answered with an even bigger smile, which was my way of saying I hoped he would tag along with me.

A few minutes later, the cute little waitress brought us our hamburgers and Cokes. Though I never tried a burger in an Oriental restaurant before, I had to admit that it was pretty darn good, and a lot better than the greasy ones back at the Warriors Den. The Golden Tiger added on the tomatoes, lettuce, onions, and pickles like there was no tomorrow. The relish and extra spices gave it a *zing,* which I never tasted before. Not only that, but they gave me a ton of French Fries, so many that I had to get a huge doggy bag to take home with me.

Anyways, by the time Eliot and me left the restaurant, I felt totally fat and bloated, to where I wondered if I could make the short walk to the house. But the sun was dropping below the mountains to the west, and the breeze got colder and colder. I wanted to get home before my poor, bare little legs had a chance to freeze worse than they already were.

Eliot and I kind-of sort-of jogged to the trailer, breathing heavier and heavier the farther we went. We exhaled steamy air from our lungs, and exchanged self-deprecating comments and laughter during our short run.

In no time, we made the corner at a state office building, crossed the railroad tracks, and soon found ourselves at the trailer, eager to get inside and warm up.

Eliot and me strolled through the cramped and cluttered living room to a hallway, passed the bathroom, Mom's bedroom, and a spare, "catch-all" room, to my sanctuary at the trailer's south end.

My room was always a mess, and the bed hardly ever made. Blankets scattered in all sorts of manners, and usually ended up on the floor. Still, I allowed Eliot into my humble little corner of the world, where I kept my computer, my posters, my pastels, and a drawer full of my artwork.

Eliot made himself at home in one corner of my queen-sized bed, as I squeezed to a shelf. There, I found a few sketchbooks, where the better stuff was stashed.

I took a deep breath, mustered my courage, handed Eliot a bunch of sketchbooks, then sat down next to him on the bed.

What happened in the next few minutes were not part of that day's plans. To make a long story short, as Eliot glanced through my artwork, he also glanced over at me. His eyes told me that he wanted something more than just a chance to peek through a few old pastels, pencil, or chalk sketches. I looked over at him, as he looked over at me.

Our lips met in a kiss.

I don't know how long that kiss lasted, but to this day I can still feel it. I kissed Eliot, he kissed me. All the while our arms wrapped around each other, in a moment of sheer magic, majesty, and bliss. Eliot was so warm, so soft, and so gentle in our embrace. I hadn't felt so good since that rainy day Danny made love to me, in the back of his cold, clammy, damp Chevy van. I only knew Eliot Munro for only about an hour or two, but it didn't matter. Any pains or regrets I suffered from my break-up with Danny O'Roarke now left me.

I ran my fingers through Eliot's dark, curly hair, gave him a couple or three wet smooches on the cheek. I told him now much I loved him, with a carefree whisper in his ear.

Once Eliot and I parted, I shut the sliding door leading to the hallway, and locked it. Mom was at work, and wouldn't be home until ten or eleven that night. Even then, I didn't want anyone screwing up what my houseguest, and apparent new boyfriend, had in mind of doing.

I already worked out of my sneakers, as Eliot got the hint and removed pieces of his own clothing. I pulled off my hoody sweatshirt, to a worn-out baseball jersey I wore underneath. I started to take off my shorts, but gave myself a moment or two to contemplate what doing so might lead to.

Eliot's eyes told me what I was already thinking, which was to take off my pants to reveal a teensy little penis which seemingly belonged on an eleven-year-old boy, and not someone who was almost eighteen. I hesitated for a few seconds, as my heart raced and my breath grew short and shallow. Panic nearly swept over me. I worried that my body wouldn't be to Eliot's liking.

Eliot's expressions begged me to remove my shorts, to show off what I had (or didn't have) underneath.

I took another deep breath, gambled that Eliot would approve of my scrawny physique the same way he did my artwork, then dared to remove my khaki shorts and *Hanes* underwear.

A split-second later, I found myself standing before Eliot Munro, wearing nothing but a worn-out baseball jersey, two-jittery eyes, a nervous grin, and a fiery blush.

A split-second after that, Eliot pulled me onto the messy, queen-sized bed, and gave me a sloppy kiss to the lips.

Eliot and I now enjoyed each other's bodies, at the south-end of an old Fleetwood trailer, on a cold, frigid November day in La Grande.

Anyways, Eliot and I never went all the way that afternoon. It still meant more to me than any of the times Danny and me lost our pants and did the nasty. As Eliot and I rolled around on my bed, we let our fingers and hands go on explorations through unknown territory. I never felt as comfortable with Danny as I did that evening with Eliot. I now knew that I had finally met *THE ONE*. Any thoughts of inferiority I suffered for being the way I was and still am no longer haunted me.

While I was still a few months away from my eighteenth birthday, I began to fully understand what it meant to be a man, in the arms of another man, which filled a once hollow emptiness that had troubled me for so long.

Whether I knew it or not at the time, I my life would never, could *never* be the same....

11

The first winter I spent in La Grande was long and horrible. All winters in northeastern Oregon are long and horrible, even when they're not. Summers are too hot, autumns are too dry, springtime's too wet, and the winters are long and horrible. Sometimes, it snows and snows and snows to the point where anyone hired to move it can't find places to put it. The snow gets so deep it caves in buildings with weak or flat roofs.

Even when the roofs are steep and the snow slides off, the white stuff is still so deep it piles up real bad along the sides of houses, where it has no room to slide off. The temperatures also get so cold, to where the snow turns into nothing but thick piles of ice.

During so-called "good winters", it might get cold, and stay down below freezing for a while. It might even get down below zero for a few days, then warm back up to the twenties. But, in bad winters, it might get down to thirty below or even worse, where pipes freeze and cars won't start. Winters that cold put people in real bad moods, because they can't take showers until their pipes thaw out, unless their pipes break and got to be fixed or replaced. And, because their cars won't start, they got to walk everywhere, bum a ride from somebody, or whine and cry to their bosses because they can't get to work, or any place else.

Every time you get outside in that cold of winter, the hairs up in your nose freezes, and you can't get warm no matter how bundled up you are, and the wind hurts every bone in your body.

Even in a warm house it gets kind of cold. The trailer Mom got was like an ice box, or a hot one, depending where you were inside it. Part of the trailer felt warm, part of it felt cold, and all you could do was just wait until the weather got hot again.

Sometimes, you'd think there was no end to winter, and you'd just sit around wondering and doubting if you'll live to see spring again.

Even though I like wearing shorts all the time, I got stuck wearing long pants, and not just because Mom fretted over me freezing my poor little legs outside. It got so cold, I had no choice but to wear long pants, which put me in a bad mood because I like wearing shorts. I even got to wearing long pants in the trailer, because it wasn't real warm in there, even though it was still warmer than it got outside.

Even when I was working on a pastel, watching TV, or hanging out with Eliot, I got real depressed because I started wondering and doubting if I'd live to see spring again, even when locals and old-timers told me that it'd come, pretty soon.

And even though most of the locals and old-timers swore up and down it wasn't a bad winter, it sure wasn't a very good one. All winters are bad, even when they're not. There's no such a thing as a good winter, no matter what locals or old-timers might say.

Anyways, it was my senior year in high school, which meant I was supposed to do a senior project in order to graduate. I had no idea what I was going to do, until Eliot came up with the idea of me doing an open house at a nearby art gallery that some of his parents' friends owned in town. Eliot talked to his parents, his parents talked to their friends who owned the art gallery, and the next thing I knew I got roped into doing an open house at the art gallery.

So, one Friday night in April, I was supposed to show off and talk to people about my artwork.

At first, I screamed and squalled and hollered and carried on like a whiny little bitch about me showing off my artwork at Eliot's parents' friends' art gallery. But the high school went along with the idea, so in order for me to graduate I had no idea but to go along.

I thought it was a terrible idea. I was afraid of getting my ass laughed out of the art gallery and prove, once and for all, what a failure I really was. I was afraid that I artwork was never and would never be worth a shit.

Anyways, I got roped into wearing my Sunday clothes on a Friday night and stand around like an idiot in the art gallery and let others tell me how bad my artwork was and that I was never and would never be worth a shit.

I was screwed.

Although the *White Dove Proudly Presents the Fantasy World of Gerald O'Fearna* thing-a-ma-jig wasn't supposed to start until seven o'clock on that Friday night in late-April, Mom and Eliot and me got to the gallery around five. Mom got the night off from work just so she could dress up in a fancy, sky-blue skirt and blouse she hadn't wore since Uncle Ray's funeral, then support her "darling little Gerry" in his moment of shining glory or tragic defeat.

I paced up and down the art gallery floor, making lame-ass stabs at humor, trying to prove that I wasn't scared when in truth I was on the verge of shitting my pants. I was more scared than right before Eliot and me first got naked and wrestled around on my bed. I was even more scared than the night when Danny and me first did the nasty. I was even more scared than I ever was giving some idiotic speech in front of school-mates, for some idiotic school project. Truth was, I don't think I was ever that scared in my entire life, even when Mom and my then-and-current-boyfriend Eliot Munro told me things were okay, and would be okay if not better.

It didn't matter what my mom or boyfriend had to say about this evening, or my artwork, or anything else at that given moment. The only opinions that mattered were those who were totally ignorant of some nervous gay kid named Gerry O'Fearna, or his crappy artwork that would never, could never be worth a shit.

Those two hours before my art show seemed to be the longest two hours of my life. Mom and Eliot kept telling me to calm down. I found myself gawking at other paintings and art displayed and for sale in the White Dove, and couldn't help but to compare my stuff to them.

Like a lot of art galleries in this neck of the woods, the White Dove had its share of paintings, pastels, and sculptures of western scenes and figures... that period of time when cowboy hats, cowboy boots, chaps, horses, cattle, and six-shooters ruled the West. Like what you saw in a lot of galleries, some of this stuff was done by hacks and phonies, Charlie Russel and Frederic Remington wanna-bes with no real originality nor talent.

On the other hand, some of this stuff was good.... *Real* good... so good that I felt jealous and envious, which only made me feel worse about myself.

One of my favorites was not exactly a *western* painting, but most definitely located somewhere in western Oregon. It involved three young boys, playing with their toy boats on a small, wooden dock. Green grass, trees, a small stream, and a bright blue sky highlighted one day in the life of these youngsters in their time of innocence and joy.

In the background, un-mistakeable in its size, majesty, splendor and glory, was the state's highest point and tallest mountain, Mount Hood.

I just had to smile at that particular painting. For me, it captured the pleasures of childhood, before the need to hold down a job, or paying bills, which pretty much ruins it for all of us. At the same time, this painting made me feel much worse about myself, which made me even more certain that my artwork would never and could never be worth a shit.

The owners of the White Dove had ordered some catering for my eventual downfall and even worse death sentence. There were a variety of drinks, finger foods, and hors'douvres for folks to snack on while they verbally ripped off my head and shit down my neck. While I paced up and down, feeling real bad about myself and my art, I tried to make a little small talk to a fat, bald, short little guy who decorated a corner table with finger steaks, hunks of celery and carrots, and some rather gross looking green stuff which no normal person would eat or even touch with their bare hands. A few soft drinks and punch were also available for those to enjoy, while they made mincemeat out of my already fragile ego.

The couple who owned the White Dove were probably in their late-thirties or early-forties, around Mom's age. David Ferguson was a nerdy-looking guy with thick, black-rimmed glasses, a receding hairline, brown hair, and a constant smirk or smartass grin on his face. Even though David's humor kind-of-sort-of-maybe put me in a slightly better mood, I wasn't sure if I liked him or not.

Elaine Ferguson, on the other hand, I liked her a whole lot, the moment her and David entered the joint from a service door near the back alley. Elaine had long, dishwater blonde hair that hung freely down below her shoulders. She had a real nice smile that made me like her, where David tried too hard to make me like him. Elaine was a tall woman, and actually a bit taller than David, though he tried to make himself look taller, and failed miserably. He also sucked in his gut to hide a pot belly, and failed miserably at that. He wasn't taller than Elaine, he never was taller, and never would he be as tall.

I liked Elaine the moment her and David showed up. She was very pretty, and also very athletic. From what Eliot told me, she was really into jogging, cycling, and weightlifting. David was really into *Monty Python* and the Marx Brothers, based on his badly delivered jokes and puns.

Anyways, Elaine carried herself with a lot of self-confidence. Ease and charm just oozed out of her. She had a real nice body that almost made me forget that I was and still am gay. She was thin where she had to be thin, with a pair of boobs that struggled to squeeze out of a blue-and-white, checkered shirt that she wore. I wondered if her tan was real, or whether she bought it at a next-door tanning salon or some other place in town. Anyways, she had a real good tan, and looked real good with it. She also had a way which made it easy to like her, even when she didn't try to make me like her, where David seemed to go out of his way to make people like him.

Thing that bothered me was that David and Elaine showed up at the White Dove, wearing shorts. *Shorts.* Both of them wore shorts, which made me uncomfortable and out of place and uncharacteristically not *me,* because I wanted to wear shorts, even when Mom told me not to because they wouldn't be nice to wear at my own art show and senior project. I wanted to wear shorts with my tie and jacket, even if they gave me a weird, *British Schoolboy* sort of look.

Mom swore up and down that it would've been wrong for me to wear shorts, so I wore the ugly black slacks which went with the tie and jacket. But then the two honchos of the White Dove had to go and show up at their place of business with short jeans, which went with their matching blue-and-white, checkered shirts. I gave Mom the evil eye, and had the sudden urge to run back home and fetch a hoody and shorts, so I wouldn't feel as dumb as I already did, or dressed up like a Christmas tree, as Uncle Ray would say.

In truth, I wanted to run off back home and put on a hoody and some shorts, then run off somewhere and hide to keep from looking dumb for all of my lousy artwork that the White Dove was showing off that wasn't worth a shit anyways.

Anyways, where David's legs were kind of pale and hairy and really not much to look at, Elaine's legs were long.... Real long, and seemed to go on forever. Like the rest of her, those two legs were tanned and shaved and shaped real nice. They almost made me forget that I was and still am gay.

Anyways, David and Elaine both walked up to Mom, smiling real big as they introduced themselves. They told how nice it was that I picked their art gallery to show off my artwork, or my lame-assed attempt at art, and how wonderful my lame-assed artwork was.

While David gave me a limp handshake, Elaine gave me a strong, firm one. She threw one arm around my scrawny shoulders and said in a husky, Lauren Bacall voice, "You have a very talented son, Mrs. O'Fearna. Gerry's going places, and we're very proud to have him as a featured artist this month."

I thought Mom was going to lose it, right then and there. Elaine kind of made me feel better about myself. On the other hand, she made Mom so happy that she began to blubber and cry and carry on and boo-hoo, almost as bad as when an old person kicked the bucket, except for different reasons. Mom got so worked up she couldn't hardly talk, so when she could talk she just sort of whispered, "Thanks, Elaine.... I always thought he was good..."

"The moment Dave and I first met Gerry, we knew he was a fine young man," Elaine went on, giving me a squeeze with a long, muscular arm, which made her look like she belonged in a "Conan" movie or something.

My face turned so red it was almost purple, not because Elaine squeezed the life out of me, but because her nice words made me feel real good, too. Like Mom, I was also kind of at a loss of words. I knew what I wanted to say. I just couldn't find the right way to say it.

The only and best way to get my idiotic feelings out were to say, "Thanks.... Thanks a lot...."

Elaine looked me and Eliot up one side and down the other and said, "You boys make such a handsome couple..."

Eliot never said much. He just smiled real big, while his face also turned funny colors when he blushed. He looked over at me in that loving way he always looked at me and let out a funny little giggle.

"We've known Eliot since he was in diapers," said David, with a sinister chuckle which made me wonder if he approved of our relationship, or was on the verge of making a snide comment about it. "I've never seen him quite this happy. Don't you agree, Elaine?"

"Eliot and Gerry need each other," added Elaine. "It wasn't luck that brought them together, but the hand of God. I truly believe that."

"By the way, Eliot," David said to my boyfriend. "Did I ever tell you of the day I shot an elephant in my pajamas?"

No matter how nervous or scared or uptight I was, I couldn't hold back the urge to give David a snotty little grin and say, "How it got in your pajamas, you'll never know."

For several seconds, David lost his own smartass grin, and was at a complete and total loss of words. He just kind of stared at me like I murdered him or something. He was in a horrible state of shock, and somehow couldn't seem to recover.

Mom, Elaine, and Eliot got wind of this, too. Mom got all scared and embarrassed, like I was about to get us all thrown out of "The White Dove Proudly Presents the Fantasy World of Gerald O'Fearna" thing, while also getting me thrown out of my dreams of becoming an artist.

Both Eliot and Elaine laughed real hard at what I had just done. They also laughed that bewildered and hurt look on David's face. Eliot slapped me real hard on the back, while Elaine gave me a high-five for ruining David's punchline.

Well, that left David standing all alone, wiping egg off his chin. He pasted on a strained, phony-assed smile, and mumbled something under his breath.

He then escaped to the other end of the gallery, to the safety of the punch, soft drinks, finger foods, hors-douvres, and those few folks who thought he was hilarious.

12

Anyways, to make a long story short, the night wasn't half-bad, and actually turned out pretty good, considering I didn't get killed or nobody said nothing too bad about my art.

Mostly, those that went there to check out the "White Dove Proudly Presents the Fantasy World of Gerald O'Fearna" thing turned out to be mainly real nice people. Oh, there were still a few who harped and hollered and whined and bitched and carried on because they wanted pictures of trees and birds and squirrels and horses and nature stuff like that. There were others who wanted to see pictures of horses, with rough and rugged cowboys on them, doing cowboy stuff in the great outdoors.... Cowboys herding cattle, cowboys drinking hot coffee around a campfire, cowboys in summer, cowboys in winter, lonely men riding alone in a vast, desolate, and empty landscape.

Anyways, like what I said before, the White Dove had more than its share of Frederic Remington and Charlie Russell hacks and wanna-bes. I was too busy trying to be a Frank Frazetta or Norman Rockwell hack or wanna-be....

Anyways, the night wasn't half-bad and actually turned out pretty good. I still spent much of the night pacing back and forth, sweating in my tie, jacket, and horrible slacks which made my legs feel claustrophobic and itchy. It didn't matter how nice people were, or how badly they wanted to see pictures of lonely cowboys and squirrels on the lone prairie.

When I wasn't busy pacing back and forth while Mom and Eliot both told me to calm down, then I mingled, answered questions, and took lots and lots of feedback from those who gave me good advice, or sometimes not so good advice. The good advice was mainly from them who accepted the art for what it was, and didn't carry on because they wanted cowboys, squirrels, trees, or snow-covered granite peaks somewhere off in the distance.

Anyways, the night turned out pretty good. I still look back on it with fondness and great memories. One good part was that David Ferguson stayed around the drinks and finger foods, and near those who pretended to act like he was funny.

I started out thinking the night would be the end of me.

Turned out it was the beginning of me as a serious artist, and maybe even as a grown-up man.

With only about an hour left to go on the "White Dove Proudly Presents the Fantasy World of Gerald O'Fearna" thing-a-ma-jig, Elaine Ferguson introduced me to an older guy who really helped me on my life as an artist.

"Gerry," said Elaine, heading toward me with a real big grin, while this older guy followed behind her, looking me up one side and down the middle. "This gentleman has taken a particular interest in your work."

I looked at Elaine kind of strangely, wondering if the gentleman in question was the older guy behind her. I also wondering what particular interest, exactly, that he took in me and my stuff. For the moment, I didn't know what to say, so I just stood there next to Eliot with a stupid look on my face. "Okay," I said, glancing over at Eliot for support, or a shoulder to cry if the particular interest in question was more naughty than nice.

"Gerry," Elaine went on. "This is Arthur O'Brien. Arthur.... Gerry O'Fearna...."

Me and this Arthur O'Brien guy just kind of engaged in a weird staring contest, wondering what one guy had in store for the other. Neither of us said much right at first. We just stared at each other, wearing nervous and awkward and stupid smiles.

This Arthur O'Brien guy was of about average height, I'd say, taller than me and a bit taller than Eliot, but not near as tall as Elaine. He had mostly gray hair that tried to point in all directions from under the Emerald green beret he wore. Arthur O'Brien had a well-trimmed and very cool mustache, which almost made me wish I could grow one. I still can't grow a mustache or much of anything else on my face, except zits. His teeth under that smile and mustache were real polished and shiny and white, like he took good care of them. They weren't dentures or anything like that, because I never saw a pair of dentures that looked so real or crookedly.

Not that I'm an expert on dentures or anything like that ...

Anyways, it wasn't just knowing that I was kind of nervous or scared. Arthur O'Brien also seemed kind of nervous or scared, like he had something important to say, and just wasn't sure in how to say it. Anyways, the way he was acting, I could tell that this guy had something in mind for me. But what, I couldn't quite tell.

"Nice.... Nice to meet you," I stuttered, looking at a couple of bright blue eyes behind a pair of steel-framed glasses and bifocals.

"Nice to meet you," agreed Arthur O'Brien. "You're a very talented artist, Gerry. Has anyone ever told you that?"

"Not the way you just did," I mumbled, nearly flattered and touched and moved to tears. I didn't know what it was, but it was obvious that Arthur really liked my stuff. It wasn't just what he said, but the way he went about saying it.

One moment, I was looking at Arthur through clear eyes. The next, I looked at him through eyes which were watery and red and sore, because I was on the verge of blubbering and boo-hooing from happiness and joy. I couldn't help my weak, wussy, wimpy, pussy, cowardly self. I tried to be tough and strong, but nearly got knocked down by the words of a kindly old gent. My eyes drifted from Arthur O'Brien, to a trashy Charlie Russell wanna-be painting, as a whimper fled from my quivering lips.

"Somewhere we can sit down and talk?" asked Arthur O'Brien, as he led me away from the comforts and safety of Eliot and Mom, over toward a couple of easy chairs and a coffee table in one corner of the White Dove, away from the noise and laughter and chatter which was David Ferguson and his cronies.

Arthur and I sat down around the table. Elaine brought us some cups of steaming hot, herbal tea, without even asking to do so.

I sat down on one of those chairs. Sweat from my shirt and jacket seemed to glom onto the black vinyl, and almost wouldn't let me go. I tried to take a drink from my tea, but it was so hot I couldn't even stand to sip it. It even burned my hand, as I touched the cup.

Anyways, as Arthur O'Brien and I sat down and got kind of comfortable, we just stared back and forth, waiting for the other guy to talk.

Finally, Arthur looked me over, squinting in a way that only those of Irish-descent can squint, and asked, "So, Gerry.... May I call you 'Gerry'?"

"Why not?" I said, on the verge of giggling. "That's my name."

Arthur smiled real big, but didn't say much right at first. Finally, he came right out and asked me, "So, Gerry.... What is it, exactly, that motivates your style and form of art?"

Without giving it a second thought, I told Arthur O'Brien of my respect and love of good ol' Norman Rockwell, and even gooder ol' Frank Frazetta.

When I was younger, my dad had a bunch of old paperback books which included *Conan the Barbarian, Tarzan of the Apes, A Princess of Mars,* and a whole bunch of other ones. Most were published by companies like *Ballantine* and *Ace Books,* which hired Frazetta to do their covers…. book covers which became classics in their own right.

Before I could even read, I spent long hours just looking at the book covers, maybe even studying or even *worshipping* them. I somehow got to wondering if I could do something like what Frazetta done.

Later, Dad passed away and Mom and me moved in with Uncle Ray and Aunt Fran, who had a bunch of coffee table books dealing with the art of guys like Maxfield Parrish or good ol' Norman Rockwell.

Had I not taken the time looking at all those books, sometimes over and over and over until the pages got badly wrinkled from fingerprints and sweat, I wouldn't have dreamed of becoming an artist when I grew up. Then I would've been afraid of growing up to be nothing, and that's probably what I would've been. *Nothing.*

"So, you credit your father's love of fantasy literature for your style of art?" figured Arthur O'Brien, rubbing his mustache as he waited for my answer.

I didn't really answer. I just sorted of nodded 'yeah'.

"Well, Gerry, I think you're very good," said Arthur, in an honest and sincere and heartfelt way.

I never said much. I just nodded out another 'yeah', and smiled in a way which said that knowing someone thought I was good made me feel better than very good. It made me feel awful good, and even better than what I normally felt about myself in a really long time.

"So, let me get to the point," said Arthur O'Brien. He leaned over toward me in his chair, and once again looked me straight in the eyes. "I'm the founder and president of the *Northeastern Oregon Celtic Society,* and I'm looking for an artist to help design our posters, pamphlets, and brochures."

I never said much. I just kind of looked over at Elaine, who smiled back at me in a way that she knew more about this whole thing than I did. Obviously, she had something to do about setting me up with Arthur O'Brien.

And Arthur O'Brien was about to make me an offer I couldn't refuse, unless I was dumber than I normally am.

"We had a very good artist for the past few years," Arthur went on, "but she's getting ready to move up to Seattle."

"Okay," I mumbled, on the verge of hearing something that was going to change my life for the better.... Or hoping I was going to hear something like that.

"This is the last year she's working as our artist," said Arthur, "so we've already got something going for our annual 'Celtic Festival' this coming August."

Arthur rested his hand on my right knee, which suddenly made me feel better about not wearing shorts, because him placing his hand on my bare legs might have looked creepy or weird. "But we need a new artist to help design our posters, pamphlets, and brochures for next year," Arthur said. He gave me a smile, which told me that he was on the verge of changing my life forever. "And the year after that.... And the year after that.... And maybe even the year after that...."

Excitement mixed with fear, as I kind-of, sort-of hoped that I was being put in a position where a 'no' on my part would've qualified me as the *Moron of the Year,* hands-down, with no suitable contenders to challenge me for that honor, award, or title.

"I can't promise you fame nor fortune, nor to even pay you for what you deserve for the amount of work I'm asking of," said Arthur, in a kind-of plea. "But I want to at least offer you the start of a brilliant career."

Arthur cleared his throat, as he thought long and hard about how to make his proposal. "I hope you understand that what I'll pay you comes straight out of my own pocket, and it's just a pittance for what someone else might pay for similar work."

Then Arthur leaned even farther forward in his chair, until his nose and mustache was less than two feet away from me. "What do you say if I agree to pay you a thousand dollars a year, for the next five years or so, for working your butt off to do some really fantastic artwork for our annual 'Celtic Festival'? You think that's something you might be interested in, Gerry O'Fearna?"

13

Anyways, to make a long story way too short, Eliot and I have been together for about six years now. I still work for the 'Celtic Society,' to do pamphlets, posters, and brochures, for their annual Celtic Festival.

When Arthur O'Brien first offered me a thousand dollars a year, I thought I'd be rich. That is, until I figured out that a thousand dollars ain't a whole lot of money. But, anyways, it's still been a real challenge and opportunity to work for that outfit, for their annual Celtic Festival.

Arthur and I don't always get along, and on more than ten occasions we've haggled, argued, and butted heads. If nothing more, at least he hasn't asked me to do Celtic cowboys, Celtic horses, Celtic lakes, Celtic squirrels, Celtic streams, lone Celtic prairies or majestic, snow-covered Celtic granite peaks.

Mainly, it's been an awful lot of fun working for Arthur O'Brien. He's referred me to a bunch of other organizations throughout the state, where I've managed to somehow make a few dollars for my artwork.

For me, after that dark and gloomy night I spent at the 'White Dove Proudly Presents the Fantasy World of Gerald O'Fearna' thing-a-ma-bob, my life took a turn for the better. I'd be lying if I said that I don't get scared and nervous anytime I show off my work. That don't ever change. When good things are said about me, I feel good. When bad things are said about me, I feel horrible and end up crying on Eliot's shoulder, until he tells me to grow a couple of balls and get over it. I try to learn from the bad things, do better the next time, and somehow move on with my life.

Although my grades weren't all that good, I graduated from La Grande High School. Eliot was still a junior, so I waited around another year for him to get his diploma. I lived at home, which helped both Mom and me, as I slowly turned into a grown-up and she got used to the idea of me being a grown-up. I got a job washing dishes and waiting tables at the Golden Tiger.

When Eliot graduated from high school, the both of us went to *Eastern Oregon University* in La Grande. During part of that time, Eliot and I paid rent to stay at Mom's trailer. I took art, while Eliot studied social work, with an emphasis on LGBT youth. When we didn't enjoy Mom's cooking, we went to the Golden Tiger, where I got an employee's discount for the best burgers in town.

Nowadays, Eliot and I share an apartment in Portland. We started new jobs, while struggling to pay the rent and bills in a crazy, unpredictable, wild, weird, and strange metropolis along the Willamette River. Eliot coaches soccer, mentors, and tutors kids, and also works for the state in social services.

I get by painting murals or a few posters here and there. Like Mom, I also became a CNA, and work for an assisted living facility. It's not easy, but it's steady.

Eliot and me ain't rich. Far from it! But I am getting a bit of attention as an artist around here in Stumpville. I haven't done any book covers or movie posters yet, but who knows? There's hope for me yet.

Anyways, Danny O'Roarke and I are kind-of-sort-of back on speaking terms. He still wants me to animate his science fiction and fantasy stories.

He teaches high school English in Springfield, and spends his weekends and holidays writing. Sometimes we get together over cups of coffee or Cokes and just talk. We just never talk about our past together.... Hanging out at parks, meeting at the Warriors Den, cuddling in the shower, or fucking in the back of his ugly old green van.

As for Mr. Brokeback Mountain.... *Jessey What's His-Name*.... I got no idea what happened to him. Neither does Danny. That guy was like three or four boyfriends ago, and buried in fading memories.

Anyways, I'm now standing in my old bedroom in that old trailer Mom and I got back on our feet in, when he first moved to La Grande. I'm in a tie, jacket, and *shorts,* getting ready for the next chapter in my life.

Despite the importance of this occasion, I still gotta wear *shorts,* even if it gives me a twerpy, British-schoolboy sort of look. I can't help it. I just gotta wear my shorts!

Mom and Aunt Fran howled, hollered, fretted, and carried on about me not wearing long pants, but I don't care. I agreed to sort of getting dolled up with the tie and jacket. But I always have and always will like wearing shorts, so I'm going to wear them for the most important day of my life.

I haven't yet saw Eliot that morning. Anyways, Mom's escorting me down the aisle, while Eliot's Mom is doing the same for him. A local justice of the peace is carrying out his duties as an officer of Union County and the state of Oregon. Invitations were sent out, a caterer was hired, and chairs and tables are set up.

At two in the afternoon, in Riverside Park, me and Eliot Munro's life together will never be quite the same.

Mom and Aunt Fran wait for me in the living room of the trailer. As I make my grand entrance, the two of them carry on about how handsome I am, and how proud they are of me. They still harp about me wearing khaki shorts, and can't help but to make a comment or ten over it. Oh, well. Mostly, we're all very happy. As we embrace, we fight back the urges to whine, whimper, bawl and boo-hoo.

Anyways, I still let go and cry like the sorry little bitch I have been, and always will be.

I sometimes wonder if Uncle Ray's looking down from Heaven, or looking up from Hell, a Henry's in one hand and a Lucky Strike in the other, his Remington cap planted firmly over his gray hair. He's probably wearing a snide, ornery grin. A few smartass remarks slip from his mouth, involving pretty Mexican women or fat negro girls. I can only hope that the old bastard's sitting back with a sly chuckle, bragging to others that maybe, just *maybe,* I'm worth a shit after all. If he can't be at this event in person, I hope he at least shows up in spirit.

Anyways, in just a couple of hours, me and Eliot Munro are getting hitched, tying the knot, jumping the broomstick....

And getting married.